I0674454

THE DARK BEFORE THE DAWN

By Annette Creswell

Outer Banks Publishing Group
Raleigh/Outer Banks

For information contact Outer Banks Publishing Group at

info@outerbankspublishing.com

Cover image by Olessya
https://pixabay.com/users/olessya-86040/

FIRST EDITION – February 2020

Library of Congress Control Number: 2020930231

ISBN – 978-1-7341687-2-3
eISBN – 978-0-4638165-5-4

Chapter One

I did not know that my life would be so profoundly changed in the drear of that late London afternoon before the world descended into the dark of war. Was it the smile in his eyes or the cleft in his chin, maybe it just was the courtesy he extended handing me the lilies and packages as I clambered aboard the bus?

I was on my way home to my flat in St John's Wood after another hectic day at St Margaret's Women's Hospital. It had been a day just like all the others, my midwifery skills being called upon to bring the babies into the world and to care for their mothers.

Tonight, I was hosting a dinner for my married friends, Audrey and Edward, who worked with me at the hospital. Audrey and I had met in nursing school from where we proceeded to train at St Margaret's. I was somewhat of a loner, my friends, Audrey and Jean seem to be all that I required. However, I was keen to be in a relationship but had been unable to find that special someone, someone who would take care of me and not use me for their own purposes.

There had been a couple of encounters, cocky young interns trying to prove their manliness one, in particular, winning me over with his charm, seducing me into his bed with exhortations of undying love. This had resulted in a hastily arranged marriage at the registry after copious amounts of gin and hot baths failed to relieve me of a six weeks pregnancy. The marriage had been traumatic, his amiability changing to disputatious soon after the wedding. He had died from a brain aneurysm two years later. After that experience, I felt rather wary of men and kept to myself. It left me wondering if my destiny was to be alone with only my friends for company and Jean would often reassure me quoting the well-worn adage: "If it's meant to be it will."

As the bus motored on through the gloom and rain, my mind reverted to that man who had assisted me in Harrods.

಄಄಄

"Charles," he had said extending a gloved hand before I boarded the bus. I presumed his wife was waiting for him at home to shower him with kisses at the door. I did not think that she would be waiting in terror as my mother had, waiting for my father to arrive home drunk, her husband, solicitor, the pillar of the community, a man who bashed his wife and did unmentionable things. *Please don't let him hurt her,* I would pray from under the blanket as the shouting and thumping would continue downstairs. I did not know if my sister used to hear them as she never commented. With her door shut and her nose in her books, she seemed to be able to ignore it all. I, however, was fraught with worry until exhausted, I would fall asleep.

It was in the morning when, apart from the mother's lack of her usual chirpiness, there was no noticeable difference in our parents' behavior. However, there was one morning when mother had stayed in bed and father had departed rather hurriedly leaving Rachel and me to throw together some bread and jam for our breakfast. We had gone to farewell her before leaving for school and as we went to plant a kiss on her cheek I noticed around her eye a large purple mark which she was endeavoring to conceal with the sheet. I do not think they were aware of the effect their fighting had on me and I wondered if I had inherited mother's trait of attracting men who had pleasure abusing women. It had left me unable to be involved in disputes however trivial.

⟡⟡⟡

I used to cherish the nights when father did not go into the pub or a court case was successful. Then we would sit peacefully in the parlor, Rachel and I with our books, mother with her knitting and father with his pipe perusing The Times. Sometimes we would listen to the music on the wireless or the nightly serials after which mother would put us to bed.

Mother and I were very close and I would look forward to coming home from school to regale her with the antics of my classmates. I thought it would put her in a good mood before father arrived home, to head off any friction which might arise if his mood was sour.

Curtailing my reveries, I peered through the condensation of the window and aware that my stop was approaching, prepared to alight. My flat was not far from the bus stop so it was not long until I was inside out of the cold. I put a match to the fire and switched on the lamps then drew the curtains. As I arranged the lilies in the crystal vase I thought of Rachel. She had been put out that grandmother had bequeathed the vase to me and had made quite an issue over it. She thought the vase should have been hers along with all the other items she had inherited. But I had stood my ground and kept it. However, she had never gotten over the fact and whenever we had spoken she had questioned me if the vase was still intact. She and I had never enjoyed a close relationship. She had and still possesses a fierce jealousy towards me. Perhaps it was the fact that she was three years older than I, doted on by the maiden aunts until I made my appearance or perhaps she saw our father taking more of an interest in me and not her. However, she was unaware that father was molesting me, sitting me on his knee, forcing my hand onto his erection then stealing into my room at night to stroke my private parts. I knew what he was doing did not seem right but he had told me it was our little secret and I was not to tell anyone especially mother. So the abuse continued until I reached puberty and was old enough to ask for a lock on my door, mother mystified why I should need such a thing. I would even endure Rachel's company and her bullying so that I would not be alone with him.

Our family home in Arundel had been bequeathed to us in equal shares. We had sold it and with the proceeds, I had leased my flat and Rachel, a professor of Egyptology had moved to Cambridge. She was a curator of Egyptian artifacts in the British Museum which necessitated traveling to Egypt and I had received a couple of postcards from her effusing about the pyramids and the tombs of the Kings. It had been in the Museum that my suspicions were raised about her amative activity with a woman. Behind a statue of Ramesses 11, I had witnessed them in a passionate embrace. It had been a shock to see her like that as I had not known her sexual proclivity. I assumed she was asexual as she did not appear interested in men as I had been. It was at Rachel's birthday dinner when I was introduced to her lover, a Miss Lucinda Goddard a secretary working for someone in the Admiralty. She was a horsey looking woman, mousy hair, thin lips slashed with tangerine lipstick and I wondered what my sister saw in her. She had said she was proposing to write a novel which left me musing if my sister would be featuring me in it however, I declined to mention that as I knew what Rachel's reaction would be.

The lilies now arranged to my satisfaction, I put away the groceries and assembled the canapés which were grapes stuffed with cheese spiked through with toothpicks. Apparently, Wallis Simpson served these at her soirees so I thought I would give them a try. After placing the beef and the vegetables into the oven I decanted the wine leaving it on the butler's tray ready to serve. I set the table and lit the candles and was pleased how they suffused the room with a warming glow. It only remained for the bonhomie of my guests to complete the setting. Then I went upstairs and ran a bath pouring in a liberal amount of bath salts. Pinning up my hair, I walked to the bedroom taking from the wardrobe the dress I would wear. It was a bias-cut sheath which fortunately had been marked half price in one of the high street boutiques. It was a perfect fit and would go well with my pearls which I kept for special occasions. Luxuriating in the froth, my mind cut again to the man who assisted me in Harrods. Apart from his sartorial splendor, there had been something else about him, something intangible, as though we had been destined to meet. What rubbish, I thought, as my toes played with the taps. It was just a chance meeting, passing like ships in the night. I put these thoughts aside and quickly dressed arranging my hair into a top knot. It was when I sprayed the perfume, I heard the doorbell ring.

My friends tumbled through the door.

"God, what a night!" commented Edward.

"Come in before you catch your deaths," I said taking their coats and umbrellas.

"Something smells good," this from Audrey as I waved them towards the fire which was now burning nicely. "It's roast beef," I replied, "But minus the Yorkshire puddings. I'm afraid I could never get the hang of those." I went to the kitchen and commenced cutting the limes for our gin and tonics. "Oh, me either," called Audrey. She and I were not noted for our culinary skills a fact which we often joked about, she telling me to marry up and have a chef or someone similar cook for me.

"Well, I'm sure it will be delicious with or without them," assured Edward taking a good swig of his drink which I had handed to him.

I took my glass and joined them on the sofa where we conversed about the goings-on at the hospital before adjourning to the table. Our rule not to talk shop on social occasions was never obeyed. The conversation always seemed to stray in that direction.

"Oh, Simpson's canapes," commented Audrey as she popped a grape into her mouth.

"Ha," I chortled, "Yes, I thought I would try them on you."

"Oh, so we are your tasters now are we Peg?" inquired Edward. "Like they used to taste for the King in case he was poisoned?"

I loved their sense of humor, the easy banter of their friendship. I sipped my drink and asked them about their upcoming trip to Scotland. They were motoring to the

Highlands where Edward was attending a medical conference and had decided to stay a few extra days relaxing and enjoying the scenery. They were staying in a beautiful hotel not far from Inverness on the River Dee. Edward said it had been highly recommended by one of his colleagues who had holidayed there with his wife. I envisaged nights in front of a roaring log fire, whiskey in hand, the scene surveyed by the stag heads adorning the walls. Edward hoped he would be able to cast a line and pull in 'the big one' as his penchant for fishing was second only to his love of golf.

Then the conversation turned to Wallis Simpson. Not about her canapés but the fact that she had snared the future King of England, the scandal of which was the subject at every dinner party in London.

"Have you read Huxley's new tome?" asked Edward as he did the honor of pouring the wine. "Aud said it had some rather good reviews in The Times, didn't you?"

"No, Ed," I replied, "I'm afraid I haven't. I've been trying to finish one of the Mitford's but am not doing so well. Working at the coal face I find I am rather whacked when I come home. All I want to do is curl up in bed with a hot water bottle and sleep."

Said Audrey, "Regarding the Mitfords, I heard the father is quite eccentric,"

"Yes," I replied, "And, pro-German. It makes you wonder if there is a war, what side would they be on?" I then wondered about Rachel. She always had an affinity with Germany and I wondered if she still held that view.

"Duff Cooper is married to one of them. Diana, I think it is," Edward added. He took another bite of the beef declaring how good it was then added, "Old Duff is high up in the Admiralty so I believe." Then I thought if Rachel's lover knew him or came across him, maybe one day I might find out. After the pudding, we continued on espousing our opinions on domestic and world events until Audrey caught me yawning.

"I think it's time we made tracks, Eddy and let Peg hit the hay."

"Oh, yes, quite right, I did not realize it was so late," said Edward escorting Audrey to the door where I handed them their coats.

"Thanks ever so, Peg," said Audrey, "It has been a lovely night and the dinner was delish."

"It was my pleasure entertaining two of my most favorite people. Do drive carefully tonight and tomorrow. The roads will be rather slippery. Have a marvelous time in the Highlands," I added kissing them both. They ran out into the night and into their car. I closed the door and commenced clearing away the detritus of the dinner. Thankfully, it had been a complete success especially the bread and butter pudding which Audrey proclaimed to have been the tastiest she had consumed in a while. It may have been because the sultanas had been marinated in a liberal amount of rum or maybe my culinary skills were improving. I placed the dirty plates and cutlery in the sink to soak. I planned to deal with it in the morning. After snuffing the candles and extinguishing the fire I headed for bed. It was not long until sleep claimed me casting me onto the shores of the following day.

Chapter Two

Thin fingers of sunlight were stealing across my eiderdown when I awoke the next day and it appeared that the worst of the weather was over. I was glad as my commute involved two changes of buses. Thinking about the washing up which awaited, I hurried downstairs to tackle it meanwhile putting an egg on to boil as well as the kettle. Then I checked if the mail had been delivered. There were the usual bills and a flyer advertising a dance at the local hall. The Times was also lying there. I picked it up noticing that Germany was announcing that all men born between 1893 and 1900 would be called up for medical inspection for suitability for military service. I hoped Germany was not thinking of rearming for another war as I made a sandwich with last night's leftover meat. The clock told me it was getting late so I dashed upstairs to brush my hair, apply some lipstick and don my uniform. I grabbed my overcoat and ran out the door just avoiding colliding with the neighbor's cat who right at that moment had decided to curl up on my mat.

An arduous journey awaited as the buses were packed and the roads slippery. There were delays everywhere and an accident had occurred near Euston Station which added to the woes of the long-suffering passengers.

I was placing my bag in the locker when Jean approached "Glad to see you arrived safely," she said,

"Oh hello there," I replied. "God, it was such a terrible trip, I thought I would never get here. Have you heard yet if there were many deliveries last night?"

"No, thank goodness, only two, the rest must have thought it was better to stay where they were until it gets a bit warmer!"

"Wouldn't blame them, last night the rain was torrential and, I added, apparently wind is forecast so we had better batten down the hatches."

"Oh, no, really? exclaimed Jean. "I will be glad when winter is over. How was your dinner last night?"

"Went without a hitch, thank goodness, but I wish I had not drunk so much. I feel a headache coming on."

"Do you want some aspirin? I think I have some in my locker."

"Thanks. That would be super." She unearthed a couple of aspirin which I gratefully took then we made our way to the post-natal ward where we were rostered on for the week. It was not long before we were confronted by matron bustling her way towards us her face a picture of anxiety.

"Ah, nurse Davis," she said, "I was looking for you. Please make sure these beds are tidied up. The corners are not up to standard and remove any stale flowers from the vases. Professor Newton is due any minute for his rounds. I don't want him to think my nurses are lowering their standards. The professor is a stickler for tidiness, as you well know."

"Certainly matron," I replied. "I was just about to start on the beds this very minute."

"Well, you had better get on with it then," she admonished "We cannot have this ward's reputation and mine sullied by a pair of slack nurses."

Jean and I scuttled around tucking in errant sheets and smoothing over covers and tried our best to make the mothers presentable.

As matron sailed off with mumblings of "the nursing profession is not what it used to be" in through the door strode the professor, a gaggle of nervous-looking interns following in his wake.

"I hope nobody asks for a pan while his eminence is here," whispered Jean.

"Neither do I," I whispered back trying to suppress a giggle. "It would be just our luck and it would really cramp his style."

The entourage proceeded to the first bed in which laid Mrs. Lynch who had undergone a cesarean operation last night. Drawing back the covers and lifting her nightdress the professor commenced inspecting the sutures he had inserted ensuring his underlings took note of the method used and advising them to always check for signs of infection. "Oi, Doc," yelled Mrs. Watts, "Can you come over "ere. Me privates are giving me the gyp and me titties are that "ard ya could bounce balls on em. Suppose that's what happens when you've had six kids. I'll be having a word to that "usband when I sees him later. He can keep that pecker of his to himself from now on and no mistake."

The professor summoned one of the interns and asked him to inspect the massive protuberances which were by now bared to all and sundry. Growing redder by the minute, the hapless fellow suggested something about placing hot water bottles on them. The professor looking superciliously down his pince-nez spluttered, "Water bottles? What poppycock! Don't you know that cabbage leaves are the best treatment for engorged breasts and frequent expressing of milk to relieve the pressure? Haven't you learned anything from your studies young man?" he railed.

"Cabbages!" screamed Mrs. Watts. "I don't want no cabbages! I'll have to get our Jackie to bring in the rabbit so he can have a good "ole chomp on me and all!" But she had not finished with her complaint as she added "And what about me privates eh? Don't tell me you're gonna stuff cabbages up there?"

She was becoming more upset and agitated and I went over to pacify her. The professor approached and tried to ameliorate the situation. "Calm yourself, dear lady," he said patting her arm, "all will be well." He turned to me and recommended salt baths to alleviate the discomfort of her nether regions.

She slunk under the covers while the occupant of the ninth bed announced, "Nursie, these laxatives you give me must have done the job! Bring me the pan now otherwise, there is gonna be an "ell of a mess in this bed!"

Jean and I doubled up with laughter raced to the sluice room.

Said Jean, "I just knew that someone would ask for a pan when the professor was on duty,"

"I know," I replied taking a clean pan from the stack. "And it would have to be that uncouth one. She would not know the meaning of discretion."

"This ward seems to be full of indiscreet people. I hope the labor ward is a bit better when we have our shift there," commented Jean.

"I wouldn't count on it. If anything it will be a whole lot worse. They will be hollering and cursing like a bunch of fishwives." Our patients were mainly disadvantaged women, women whose husbands would more often than not be in a pub drinking away their wages or impregnating their wives with numerous offspring.

Pan in hand, I arrived just in time to avert a disaster and noticed that the professor had swanned off with his minions to another ward. We tended to the needs of the mothers, taking temperatures, sorting out problems with cracked nipples and writing up the charts. Mrs. Watts had settled down to have a nap, no doubt dreaming of cabbages!

Then after washing down the tiles in the bathroom, polishing the sterilizers and the brass plates at the end of the beds, it came time for a well-earned break. We made our way to the tearoom and found a couple of unoccupied chairs into which we fell glad to be off our feet for a while. Jean offered to get our tea which usually tasted stewed but at least it would be hot and reviving.

"Ah," commented Jean as she gave me the tea. "It's good sit down after such a hectic morning."

"It certainly is." I agreed.

"What do you have on yours, anything interesting?" I asked glancing at her sandwich.

"No, just the usual, cheese and pickle, you?"

"Last night's leftover beef. Mustn't let good food go to waste."

We sat in companionable silence eating our sandwiches and enjoying the break and then I found myself telling her about my encounter in Harrods.

"I was so embarrassed Jean. We bumped heads when he was helping me pick up the money I had dropped under the counter. He seemed to think it was rather humorous and then he proceeded to carry my bags to the bus stop. He was so courteous. There seemed to be something about him that piqued my interest and he has been on my mind ever since. It's a bit silly of me really. He probably has a lovely wife at home and I shall never set eyes on him again."

Jean put down her cup and meeting my gaze said philosophically, "One never knows where cupid will sling his bow, Peg, stranger things have happened."

Her words were reassuring but I knew the thought of him would not leave my mind easily.

Changing the subject I remembered the advertisement in the mail.

"I saw a dance advertised at the hall not far from my place. Do you fancy going?"

"When is it on?"

"In a few weeks,"

"Righto," replied Jean, "Sounds super. We will put on our glad rags and have some fun."

We took our cups to the table and discarded the greaseproof wrappers of the sandwiches into the bin, then made our way to the lavatory wherein the mirror our veils were straightened and fresh lipstick applied. Pleased we were now up to matron's standards we returned to the ward for another shift.

Visiting time was between 4.00 and 5.00 pm when the wards would be invaded by hordes of relatives and friends all anxious to see the patients and their offspring. We did not look forward to these times as it was not conducive to the orderly routine we had established. Unruly children would tear around with harassed fathers doing their best to rein them in. Mothers would chastise their husbands either for not being on time or neglecting to bring them their favorite sweets. Many an argument would ensue and we would have to intervene to bring some semblance of order.

Mr. Dunn had arrived with his brood of five. The youngest one with jam smeared face was in the process of clouting one of his sisters who was giving as good as she got. The others were playing hide and seek under the beds and to our consternation, one managed to knock over a vase sending the flowers and water all over the floor.

Mrs. Brown was regaling her sister about what had transpired this morning.

"Hey, Ethel, I caused a right ruckus in 'ere when his nibs came on his rounds. I got the pan just in time and the old boy had to cover his nose and took 'orf right smart. It was such a hoot and no mistake," she guffawed, her chesty laugh attesting to her overindulgence of cigarettes.

Finally, visiting time ended and the invaders had departed. It was time for us to return to the ward to some form of normality. The babies were due for their feeds so Jean and I made our way to the nursery to collect the tiny bundles who were now noisily demanding their milk. Soon they were all suckling well except for one new mother who was having difficulty getting her baby to latch on to the nipple. I showed her the technique and soon baby got the hang of it and was sucking away like all the others. Our shift now drawing to a close, we made sure the mothers were comfortable before handing them over to the night nurses. Mrs. Watts was becoming used to the cabbage leaves covering her breasts and following professor Newton's advice the expression of milk had helped a great deal. Even the salt baths she looked forward to with relish. "This "ole salt does the trick for me privates nurse," she had told me as she had happily sat in the bath. "I just 'ope you don't run out of it." I put her mind at rest assuring her there was a plentiful supply and was pleased it was relieving her discomfort.

"Bye, Peg, have a good trip home. Hope it will be a better day tomorrow," wished Jean as we left to catch our respective buses.

"Same to you and thanks ever so for the aspirin, I would have had a stinker of a headache otherwise."

"No problem, anytime," she shouted boarding the 34 bus which had pulled up at the stop.

My journey home was uneventful, and I managed to grab a window seat. I was looking forward to some hot soup, a long soak in the bath, a bed warmed by a hot water bottle and my book which was begging to be finished.

Chapter Three

The next weeks passed in a blur of activity and now it was time for a bit of fun and relaxation at the dance. Audrey and Edward had returned from their stay in Scotland and by all accounts, had an enjoyable time. Edward had been quite chuffed that he had managed to land a huge salmon which had been cooked for their dinner by the head chef. Also, the weather had improved during their stay enabling them to take brisk walks in the Highland air. Now they had to settle down into their normal routine after being used to a period devoid of alarm clocks.

"Peg, oh you do look smashing!" this from Jean as we prepared to leave my flat. "Love that dress. Blue suits you with your dark hair." I had chosen to wear my blue chiffon and had let my hair down as it was usually tucked under my cap. "Oh, ta," I did a little curtsy. "You've scrubbed up alright too," I replied putting on my coat and closing the door.

We had elected to walk as the night, although cold, was clear and there was a moon lighting the way. As we strolled, I thought about who might be at the dance and if there would be people we had not met before. Usually, they would be the same old faces. It would be nice to meet someone different.

"Have you caught up with any news lately?" Jean asked. She had stopped to release a pebble from her shoe."I noticed something in The Times," I replied "about Germany wanting men to be medically inspected for suitability for military service. I hope they are not thinking about instigating another war."

"Oh, I could not bear it either," replied my friend. "After the depression and the Great War, it does not bear thinking about." Jean was rather a worrier and I did not want to say more to add to her concerns. I said as cheerfully as I could,

"Well, we won't think about any of that tonight. We are going to enjoy ourselves."

ജ്ഞാഗ്ഞ

Arriving at the hall we noticed a few people from the hospital. It seemed that my hunch was right. There were not many new attendees and those that were looked to be rather aged. Robert, an anesthesiologist enquired if I would like a lemonade and we proceeded to the table where the drinks were obtained. I noticed Jean already on the floor being twirled around by a portly ruddy-faced fellow who was old enough to be her father. The look on her face signified she would love to be rescued. Poor Jean, I hoped she would meet someone nice tonight as she had been recently jilted and had not taken it very well.

"Would you be a sport?" I said to Robert "And cut in on Jean's partner? She looks as though she needs a bit of help."

"No problem," replied Robert. "On one condition, that you have the next dance with me." He threaded his way through the throng and broke up the ill-matched couple. Keeping my promise, Robert and I took to the floor for the next dance which happened to be the Lambeth Walk. It was so much fun, the latest dance from America, and everyone enjoyed it. I thought the band was not at all bad considering they were only local musicians. Their repertoire contained all the latest tunes.

"Phew, thanks Robert," I said as the dance ended. "That was super. I think I shall sit out the next one and catch my breath if you don't mind." Ok, that is fine by me. Would you like another drink in the meantime?"

"That would be lovely, thank you."

I made my way to a vacant chair and through the crowd noticed a couple at the far side of the hall. The woman was heavily pregnant and, to my astonishment, the man beside her was the one who had assisted me in Harrods. He looked in my direction and I found myself blushing and in somewhat of a quandary. I knew he would be married and a child on the way. I could not decide what to do but decided out of politeness I should go and greet them however they were on their way over to me.

"Hello, I thought I recognized you," said he. "If I'm not mistaken you were the damsel in a bit of bother a few weeks ago."

Said I, "Oh, hello. I thought I recognized you too."

He extended a hand.

"Allow me to introduce my wife Diana Davenport."

I already knew his name was Charles that was why he did not mention it now.

"Hello, I am Peggy Davis," I replied hoping my voice did not belie what I was feeling.

"So pleased to meet you," I said extending my hand towards her but it was not reciprocated instead she cast her eyes over me, appraising me. There appeared to be evidence of boredom as though she wished she was somewhere else.

"Your husband very kindly came to my rescue in Harrods," I explained.

"Oh?" she replied.

"Yes, it was rather embarrassing actually. He helped me pick up some money I had dropped and then carried my packages to the bus stop."

As the words fell from my mouth I thought it made me appear rather foolish and clumsy. I found it hard to imagine her acting like that. With her perfectly applied makeup and coiffed hair she appeared so prim and proper I regretted saying what I did. I changed the subject.

"Do you usually attend these dances?" I asked.

Before she had a chance to reply Charles cut in, "No, as a matter of fact, Di and I just popped in to see one of my old friends who plays the sax for a hobby. He wanted us to hear him play so, as we were in town, I thought, why not?"

"We are staying in our pied a Terre at the moment," Di added. I could sense she wanted me to know how wealthy they were and also why her husband should be associating with someone as lowly as I.

I refused to let her animosity upset me.

"I see you are expecting," I said casting a warm smile towards her. "And may I offer you both my congratulations. Actually, I am a midwife at St Margaret's. I don't suppose you are booked in there?"

She bristled, "Oh no, my confinement will be at Chatsworth House, a private facility in Knightsbridge."

"Oh well, I'm sure you will receive the best care and everything will go well."

The band had stopped for their break. Charles made their excuses and escorted his wife over to meet his friend the sax player. Still reeling from meeting him and the frosty reception from his wife I sought out Jean to tell her what had transpired. I found her in the lavatory fixing her hair.

"What?...him, here? Blimey, what were the chances?" she gushed incredulous at the news.

"I know, I could hardly believe it myself." I surveyed my face in the mirror. I needed to see if there still remained a blush on my cheeks.

"You thought he was married," said Jean as we walked towards the hall.

"Yes, I was right about that wasn't I? But I have to say his wife did not come across as very friendly."

"Well, she probably thought he had designs on you. After all, he did go out of his way to help you and you are certainly attractive."

I let that slide. He did not seem that type at all. He had only been courteous towards me. Just like a true gentleman would behave. I thought of David, my late husband, and could not visualize him going out of his way to help me let alone a stranger.

"Do you want to grab our coats? I asked as we entered the hall "I think I have had enough excitement for one night and I am feeling rather knackered."

Jean agreed and as we were standing at the coat counter Charles and Diana came over. I introduced them to Jean and watched if Diana's attitude was the same towards Jean as she had shown to me. It was a bit more genial although there was a discernible condescension.

Then Charles offered us a ride home. Jean and I looked at each other. It would certainly save us the walk back and I was feeling a blister forming on my toe, the result of the new shoes I had been foolish to wear. We soon found ourselves reclining on beige leather seats in the back of Charles' car. Although the journey was not very long, I discerned from the conversation that Charles had an interest in antiques and fine arts which necessitated travel abroad. It brought to my mind Rachel on her jaunts to Egypt probably with her lover in tow. Diana went on to say that as there was a forthcoming trip to France and she was due in a few weeks she had enlisted her mother's assistance as a back- up in case Charles was absent. During the ride, I could not resist regaling them with our funny experiences on the ward one, in particular, had Charles laughing uproariously. However, there was nary a sound or comment from his wife.

"I thought a hospital was supposed to be a dull place but I think you have changed my mind on that score!" he managed to say through his mirth.

As we approached Jean's house Diana spoke again. She mentioned a title and an estate in Bedfordshire. Jean and I looked at each other with eyebrows raised. I certainly was not far off the mark with his Saville Row suit I mused as Jean alighted.

"Thanks ever so much for the ride home," I said climbing from the car. "My feet certainly appreciated it. I do hope all goes well for you Diana. It was lovely to meet you. Goodbye Charles, and thanks once again."

As I walked to the gate and watched the car drive off into the night I thought that would be the last time I would see them however I did not know what fate had in store.

Chapter Four

The passing weeks saw an increase in births and referrals as St Margaret's was the main teaching hospital in London. Audrey had been rostered on to the labor ward and was quite chuffed to be seeing Edward through the day, albeit sporadically. We were rushed off our feet giving enemas, checking dilations of cervixes and encouraging and supporting our charges in their times of need. It suited me to be busy, to keep memories at bay, memories I tried to store in the back blocks of my mind.

"Nurse Davis," called matron popping her head around the door of the sluice room, "Could you please go to Admissions? A Mrs. Morton has just come in and may need a wheelchair."

"Certainly, right away Matron," I responded hastily emptying a pan. After washing my hands I adjusted my veil and scanned the ward for a chair. I found one lurking in the corner. Quickly I maneuvered it out of its hiding place and wheeled it along the corridor to Admissions.

There I encountered an anxious husband, suitcase in hand doing his best to placate his distraught wife.

"Oh, it hurts so much, Georgie, and I think I have wet myself too. What will it be like when I have to deliver our baby?" She clutched his arm, a look of terror on her face.

"Don't worry, dearest?" he told her. "I'm sure the nurse here will take good care of you."

"Yes, you can be sure of that," I said. "I am nurse Davis and you are?"

"George Morton and this is my wife Dorothy."

I assumed a business-like approach.

"Pleased to meet you, now, let's get Dorothy into the chair and don't worry about the mess. It means that her waters have broken so it won't be long until you have your baby." With her husband's help, I guided her into the chair, her plaintive cries still continuing.

"Now, say goodbye to your wife and I will take her to the ward."

George gave her a peck on the cheek and told her to do as she was instructed. I summoned a porter on duty who carried the suitcase and, with Dorothy squirming in pain we made our way to the labor ward.

"I can't wear this," she protested. "Everyone will see my backside."

I had handed her the regulation hospital gown which opened at the back not affording the wearer much modesty.

"Can't I wear the new nightie I brought?"

"No, I'm sorry but everyone has to wear these gowns.," I told her. "They are standard hospital issue and are more practical for medical examination. I'm afraid that modesty tends to go by the wayside when one is giving birth."

"Alright then," she acquiesced grimacing as another contraction surfaced. "I suppose I will have to put up with it."

"That's the spirit," I called to her. I was in the process of locating a pan and the enema apparatus and knew that the procedure would not be favorably received.

"Now just relax," I advised inserting the tube "This will be over in a jiffy."

"Ow, oh sorry, but I hate this. No one told me all this would happen. Ow, the pain is getting worse. Can I have something to make it go away, please?" I won't be able to stand it much longer," she cried.

"Now calm down. I will take a look and assess how many centimeters you have dilated and then we will fetch the doctor if need be."

"Oh, please hurry. I can't bear it and I need to push." She was writhing on the bed.

"Stay still."

I managed to ascertain that her cervix had dilated to five centimeters and decided to summon of the obstetricians.

Richard came quickly bringing with him Robert the anesthesiologist with whom I had danced at the hall. After assessment Richard agreed it was time to deliver, telling me quietly that it would be a forceps job. Robert placed the mask over her face and delivered the chloroform. It did not take long until a downy head emerged to greet the world and, to everyone's relief, a lusty cry of the baby boy filled the room.

"Phew, it's certainly busy. Haven't had time to catch my breath," exclaimed Jean plonking herself down in one of the chairs. We were having our usual break in the tea room.

"I wish they would have some decent tea," I whined, "this always tastes stewed."

"That will be the day," responded Jean. "They probably think if we have good tea we will spend more time in here drinking it." "Have you got a gasper only I seem to be fresh out."

I handed her one of my cigarettes which she lit.

She took a good puff and settled back in the chair then looked across at me.

"You know, I just heard from one of the nurses in Emergency that a young girl was just admitted with a botched abortion. Apparently, she had been abused by her stepfather and this was the result. She had used a knitting needle and was found hemorrhaging on the bathroom floor."

"Oh, the poor little thing," I replied "I can't understand how men can do such shocking things. I hope they jail him for the rest of his life."

As the words left me, memories surfaced of being rushed in an ambulance to the Emergency department of

Brighton hospital as blood containing the twelve-week old fetus drained from my womb. David kept repeating how sorry he was, David, my husband, the intern, the soon to be doctor, he, who would take the Hippocratic Oath vowing not to do harm. Mother was the only one who had been privy to that, taking me in, telling father that I had suffered a miscarriage. Thankfully Rachel was living on campus in Cambridge so she was not there to rub my nose in my disastrous marriage. It was enough that I had upset mother indulging in premarital sex. "Oh, Peggy," she cried, "I thought we had brought you up better than that. What were you thinking letting things get out of hand? Didn't you know it is the woman who should call a stop to a man's passion?" She did not know that David had told me he would take care of everything. "Darling I am nearly a doctor," he had said as he entered me. Silly naive Peggy, believing the lies he was telling so his needs could be assuaged.

Mother tried to warn me off him. I think she must have had a sense of what he was capable of but as I was pregnant, marriage was my only option. Father had never known of the pregnancy as a mother and I made a pact we would not tell him. If he had known that David had impregnated me he would have possibly been jailed for manslaughter. During my recuperation at home, David had attempted to see me but mother would not open the door. She was concerned for my welfare and probably her own.

"You coming?" asked Jean "You looked miles away."

Abandoning my grim memories, I drained the last dregs of tea and extinguishing my cigarette went with Jean to face the remaining hours of our shift. She went off to the antenatal and I decided to pop into the nursery to check on Dorothy's infant. As I passed by Emergency, I heard the screams of a woman. "Oh, please, you must do something." Overcome with curiosity, I entered the room to find Edward hovering over a patient, a distraught older woman by her side.

"Ah, Peggy," exclaimed Edward, "another pair of hands. This patient was knocked down by a car and is in a very bad way," he explained. "Can I enlist your help?"

"Of course," I said mentally hoping that I would not be needed by the matron. I walked over to the bed and was shocked to find that this patient was none other than Charles' wife Diana.

"Oh," I exclaimed, "I know her."

The older woman her face mottled with anxiety and tears clutched my arm, "Oh please can you do something? I am Cecily and you apparently know my daughter." She managed to inform me that her son in law was due to arrive soon.

Diana was covered in blood. It was spurting from an artery in her left leg which was pointing in entirely the wrong direction. I raced to the cupboard and grabbed a mask and scrubs.

"I will have to perform a cesarean section," said Edward. "I can hardly detect the fetal heartbeat. There is no time to waste." He summoned the anesthesiologist who had been standing by.

"Doctor Sullivan, please administer the anesthetic now, there is no time to transport this patient to the labor ward."

He told me to keep checking her pulse and to keep the sponges coming.

"Damn, I can't seem to stem this hemorrhage!" Edward cried as I handed him more sponges.

Charles burst through the door.

"Oh, Diana."

He went to approach but Cecily pulled him back and they hovered in the background as we tried to save mother and child. I focused my attention on the task in hand and was pleased I had the mask over my face. It served to hide what I was feeling. Here he was in my midst with his wife dying and probably his baby as well.

Finally, the bleeding was stemmed. The anesthetic was administered, and iodine was applied to Diana's swollen belly. As Edward commenced the incision I was aware that we were all standing on a blood-soaked floor. Diana's face took on a deathly pallor and I noticed her pulse was becoming weaker. After a few minutes, a silence descended on the room as the still-born girl was extricated from Diana who lay comatose on the bed. Cecily fell into Charles' arms, crying inconsolably. I cut Edward a glance of sympathy as he had done all that had been possible in the circumstances. Taking off my mask I went over to Charles and Cecily to offer words of comfort which I knew would be rather meaningless at this terrible time. My eyes were filled with tears as I thought of Charles' dead wife and also his baby daughter.

"I'm so sorry, Charles. If there is anything I can do, please let me know."

He replied wiping his eyes with a handkerchief. "Thank you, Peggy. It was so good that you were here assisting in her final hour. She would have appreciated it."

I led them through to an annex adjoining the Emergency.

"It isn't very luxurious," I explained, "But at least you can sit in privacy and have some tea and a biscuit." Oh, and there is a chaplain who I could summon to see you if you like."

They looked at one another uncertainly each attempting to elicit agreement. Then Charles nodded. Yes, they would see the chaplain. I left them there in that tiny room in which they both looked completely out of place especially Cecily who, still in grief seemed to possess the same haughty attitude as her daughter. Must not think ill of the dead, I mused as I located matron and the chaplain advising them of the situation. The chaplain walked with me to the annex and then we accompanied Charles and Cecily to the little chapel, the room off which lay Diana and her baby girl. It was all so terribly sad and I asked God to give them the strength to cope with the tragedy they had just endured.

Outside the hospital, Charles told me the full story, how the accident occurred. Diana and her mother had been shopping for things for the baby and Diana had slipped off the curb. She had been hit by a car that did not have time to stop. The driver had been treated for shock at the scene as had Cecily. It had all been a tragic accident with no one at fault. He said he would let me know when the funeral would be held and if I wished to attend. I had not expected this but found myself accepting and giving him my address. His face etched with grief, he shook my hand in farewell. He took his mother in law's elbow and escorted her to the car which ultimately would take them to Bedfordshire. I turned and walked back to the hospital hardly able to comprehend all that had transpired in the last few hours.

That night my mind was in turmoil. I could not stop thinking about Charles. How he must be feeling to lose his wife and child in such a short space of time. I lay awake for hours eventually to doze off just when the birds commenced their dawn chorus. Thank heavens today was Saturday and I did not have to go to the hospital as the way I was feeling I was certain I would not have coped. I had a bath then went downstairs to prepare breakfast while through the window I noticed the day was fine. Enjoying my egg and toast my thoughts turned to the washing begging to be done, the cleaning of the flat and the grocery shopping. At least the chores should dissuade me thinking about Charles and his tragedy. Also, tonight, Jean and a friend of hers had asked me to see a new film starring Fred Astaire. It had some good reviews and if nothing else would hopefully give me something more cheerful to think about.

Chapter Five

I was at Euston station waiting for the train to take me to
Millbrook to Charles' home at Hagley Hall as I had
received on Wednesday a rather formal envelope with a
Bedfordshire postmark. It had been a note from Charles
notifying me of Diana's funeral, which was to be held on
Friday at their private chapel followed by a wake at the
house. It also stated that as it was a long journey, I would
be welcome to stay in one of the guestrooms for the
night. I had been rather taken aback by this but reasoned
it was the only practical thing to do. It was quite a way
and I would have to spend the night somewhere. He had
left a telephone number for me to contact him to advise
him of my attendance. I had nervously dialed the number
and had spoken to his butler Hudson who had put
Charles on the line. We had exchanged pleasantries. I had
asked him how he was and how he was coping. I was
rather at a loss to know what to talk about as I barely
knew him and what does one say to someone who had
just lost one's wife and child. He had paused to cough

once or twice and I wondered if he had caught a cold. The conversation ended with instructions for me to catch the six-thirty from Euston to Millbrook at which station his chauffeur Bill would collect me.

ഇര്ധ

The porter placed my suitcase in the luggage van and I boarded the train managing to secure a compartment with a seat near the window. I settled back to enjoy the journey and the scenery which I knew would be delightful after we left the outskirts of London. I thought about Hudson, the butler. I had never been waited on by such a person and I wished it could have been under happier circumstances. I wondered if there would be a maid catering to my needs. I would prefer to look after myself. I really did not relish some stranger poking through my things, assessing the state of my underwear which was in need of replacement. We had been traveling for about forty-five minutes when we stopped at a station and my reverie was jolted by a large lady encumbered by a variety of bags attempting to squeeze through the compartment door. She then plonked herself in the seat next to me.

"Ere, love," she hollered, "All right if I sit here? Me feet are killin' me. I 'ad to walk to the station as I missed the bloomin' bus, then I nearly missed the train and I 'ad the devil of a time carryin' me bags and all me bits and bobs." She reminded me of my patients at the hospital, especially Mrs. Watts.

ഇൗഇൗഇൗ

"Where ya 'orf to love?" she inquired.

"I'm going to Bedfordshire," I replied not wanting to engage in conversation. I just wanted to be with my thoughts, to relax and look at the scenery.

"Oh, that's nice. "I 'ad a cousin livin' round those parts," she replied my short reply no deterrent to her loquacity. "Or was it Gloucestershire, "I can't remember. Would ya like some sandwiches? I made 'em last night. Never trust the food on these trains and the cost. It would leave you broke for a week and no mistake!" She continued on and to make matters worse proceeded to spill the thermos of tea over us.

"Oh, sorry, lovey, I am a silly billy."

It was the last straw! I collected my handbag and rushed to the lavatory in an attempt to clean my skirt praying there would not be a stain. Using some soap which had seen better days I rubbed it with my handkerchief until it was barely noticeable. Stupid woman! I fumed hoping she would soon get off the train. However, when I returned I noticed she had thankfully vacated to another compartment and had spread herself about with her paraphernalia to annoy some other passengers. Thank goodness, now I was able to relax and continue my journey in peace. I gazed through the window. The urban sprawl had now given way to green fields dotted with fat sheep. My mind kept going over the events of the past weeks and I could not imagine how

Charles would be feeling. I was not looking forward to the funeral. It would be so heartbreaking for everyone involved. I was also apprehensive about staying at such a grandiose establishment and having to deal with the staff who worked there and I again thought of Hudson, the butler. However, as it was only for one night I decided to make the most of the experience as I probably would not have another opportunity.

In a cloud of steam, the train pulled up at Millbrook. I alighted and claimed my bag from the porter who had removed it from the luggage van. I walked through the exit and spotted a large black car pulling up on the other side of the station. The driver's uniform and cap alerted me he was the chauffeur. I went over.

"Good morning," he said as he climbed out of the car "I am Bill and you, I presume, are Peggy Davis."

"Yes," I replied, "Hello Bill. Thank you so much for collecting me."

He expertly placed my suitcase on the back of the car and opening the back door ushered me in.

We drove off.

"Did you have a good trip from London?" he asked as he changed gears. "Yes, thank you. It was not too bad considering." I thought I would keep the details of my mishap to myself.

I settled back in the seat. It had the same leathery smell and I knew this was the same car which Charles had driven the night of the dance.

ഇഇഇ

We traveled through tiny villages nestled in valleys as quaint thatched-roof cottages and dry-stone walls added to the charm of the scene. En route, I asked Bill about the house and if there was a lot of staff. "There used to be," he replied glancing at me in the mirror, "however, because of the depression quite a few of the maids and Charles' valet had to be let go and there is now only one groomsman at the stables." He went on to say that the depression had left big estates such as this in quite a difficult financial position and the cost of maintenance and taxes were very high. He inquired how I knew Charles and I explained to him how we had simply met by chance and that I had been with his wife in her final moments. He told me that Charles was the son of lord Davenport, who was deceased and had left the estate to him, the only son and heir. Charles also owned a pied-a-terre in Kensington which he used whenever he was overseeing the antique shop in which he had an interest. I thought about Diana mentioning that, the bolt hole in London. My mind was reeling with all this information and butterflies took flight in my stomach. Charles was lord of the manor! My nervousness was increasing with every passing mile.

Huge iron gates appeared. We drove through them and along a private road which was lined at either side with giant beech trees. In the distance I discerned chimneys and as we came closer, replete with turrets and leadlight windows this gorgeous Tudor manor house was before us. The gravel of the driveway crunched under the wheels as Bill brought the car to a stop.

"Here we are then," he announced. "Welcome to Hagley Hall." He opened the door and I stepped out to be greeted by Charles, Cecily, a man I presumed to be Hudson the butler, and two English setters who instantly ran over and tried to jump on me their fluffy tails wagging with friendliness.

"Algie, Byron, down boys, heel," admonished Charles as he tried to control them. "Sorry about that Peggy. They tend to get excited when guests arrive."

"Oh, that's alright," I replied, "I love dogs especially ones like these."

Charles did not look well. There were dark circles under his eyes and he was coughing occasionally. He was in need of a good rest. Cecily approached and we exchanged a hug. She also looked quite drained. I offered them both my sympathy. I was at rather a loss about saying anything more. I could see they were under a great strain and would be glad when the day was over. Hudson carrying my suitcase led the way inside. We entered an entrance hall our feet echoing on the marble floor and high above there was a painted vault of ceiling carved with gilded Tudor roses. We walked along a huge corridor the walls of which were hung with various portraits which I presumed were Charles' ancestors. My room, which was on the third floor was very much to my liking. With its blue and white Liberty wallpaper and a four-poster bed, the window looked out over the gardens which were presently being tended by a gardener. I commenced unpacking and putting away my clothes. There was a lovely Queen Anne dressing table on which I arranged my brush, perfume, and cosmetics. As I was attending to that there was a knock at the door. I opened it to be greeted by the housekeeper who introduced herself as Mrs. Keen. She informed me that the funeral would commence in an hour and to make my down to the drawing-room. From there we would make our way to the chapel. She indicated that it was to be a private service attended by close friends and family and, by the tone of her voice and attitude I think she was wondering why I had been invited. I asked her where the location of the drawing room was as I did not wish to make a fool of myself and be caught wandering around the labyrinth of rooms. She gave me directions and also the location of the bathroom then, nose in the air, she swanned off. I did not take to her at all.

I had packed a black suit which I surmised would be appropriate and, after placing it on the bed, went to locate the bathroom to freshen up. I clipped on my earrings, applied more lipstick and ventured downstairs to meet the other mourners.

After somber pleasantries had been exchanged Hudson announced that it was time to leave.

"Thank you, Hudson," Charles replied after another fit of coughing consumed him.

We filed out of the drawing room and I was accompanied by Cecily for which I was grateful as I did not know anyone else there. Some fellow had introduced himself as Bunny who purported to be an old friend of Charles. They had known each other at Oxford and had been in the same rowing team and had amassed a few trophies in their time. He was an affable sort although his familiarity seemed a little overbearing. However, he had put me at ease and for that I was grateful.

ಬಡಬಡ

Adorned with pink and white roses the single coffin stood at the foot of the altar while flickering candles illuminated the stained-glass window depicting the scenes of the bible. We knelt down in the pews as the Minister commenced the service. My head bowed, I prayed for Diana and her daughter and for God to give strength to Charles and Cecily. I had not attended many funerals apart from my parents and a couple of aunts who had succumbed to old age. Father had died first. A coronary occlusion had taken him as he was on his way home from the office, the news being brought to our door by the local policeman. I remember mother answering the knock thinking that it was father, late again, his key lost in the carousal of the pub. I can see her face, the anger replaced by shock and our neighbor prevailed upon to put my sister and me to bed while mother's needs were tended. My reaction to his death had been a relief, relief that I would no longer have to feel unsafe in

44

my bed and in the house, relief that I would no longer have to feel his hands crawling over me. However, mother had been quite grief-stricken at his demise. Years later, dying from liver cancer, she had whispered to Rachel and I that for all our father's faults he was the only man she had truly loved. This had been the only time mother had confided in us. I think because she knew her time was near she wanted to clear the air, make peace with herself and let us know our parents really loved each other. I had thought would she still have loved him as much if she had have been aware of the abuse he had perpetrated on me his baby daughter. What would have been her fate and mine if I had told her what he had been doing?

I was brought sharply back to the present by a commotion in the chapel. I looked over and noticed that Charles had collapsed to the floor. Bunny and another man were helping him to his feet. He looked ashen. The minister hurriedly concluded the service and I went over to lend whatever assistance I could. Charles was escorted back to the house and laid on the chaise-longue. I located Mrs. Keen and requested some smelling salts which were promptly brought and placed under Charles' nose to revive him. I felt his forehead which was hot to the touch and, as he was still coughing, I diagnosed a bad dose of influenza. I looked around for Cecily to convey my suspicions but I assumed she would be still in the chapel with the Minister so it was Hudson I told who fetched the doctor.

While the mourners were directed to the garden for refreshments the doctor was summoned, and a fellow called Tims managed to help Charles up the stairs to his bedroom. I followed a little way behind and waited until Hudson returned and Charles had been undressed and put to bed. I lingered outside the door until I was permitted to enter. I stayed with Charles trying to give him some sort of solace in his ill and distressed state. I located the bathroom in which I found a towel. Wetting it I placed it on his forehead until the doctor arrived then I made my way downstairs where Hudson and a footman were bringing out sandwiches from the kitchen. I was directed out to the garden to join the others for a drink which I was now in dire need of.

"What ho," exclaimed Bunny sidling up to me drink in hand, "I say, that was a spot of bad luck, the lord out for the count. Have they rung the doctor?"

I bit into a sandwich or what passed for one. It was a tiny triangle of bread with the crusts cut off and tasted of chicken with a touch of mayonnaise.

"Yes," I replied, "They have and I think he will diagnose a case of influenza."

"Oh, so are you a medico?" he asked eyebrows raised quizzically. Cutting him a look I replied,

"No, I am a nurse, a midwife actually."

"Jolly good," he said, "terrible tragedy, what?" Old Charlie is having quite a time of it."

☙☙☙

I started to respond when Cecily came hurrying over her face a portrait of anxiety.

"Oh Peggy, there you are," she nodded at Bunny who was helping himself to another glass of wine.

"It is one thing after another," she said hardly able to catch her breath. "Mrs. Keen has just had word that her sister has fallen ill with influenza and there is nobody to look after the children. She is catching the train within the hour. What are we to do? We will be short-staffed with her absent and with Charles ill how are we to manage?" Her distress was acute and I noticed her eyes welling.

"Something will turn up, old thing," this from Bunny whose jollity was lost on Cecily.

Feeling rather helpless, I told her I would go and see if the doctor had arrived. It would give me something to do instead of standing around eating and drinking as though it was a wedding and not a wake.

Replied Cecily, "Oh, yes that would be good of you dear, and see if you can track down Hudson, he should know something. Ask one of the staff if you cannot locate him. Now I must go and attend to the guests." She bustled off taking her concerns with her.

Leaving Bunny to his third drink I went back to the house and found Hudson talking to the doctor. He had just examined Charles and had confirmed my suspicion that he was suffering from influenza and because of his run-down condition required lots of bed rest. He had left a sedative and aspirin for him to take and we were to ensure he drank plenty of liquids. As he was shown out he added that he would look in again tomorrow to check on his condition.

"Well," muttered Hudson running a hand through his sparse gray hair. "This is indeed a dark day. I will have to let her ladyship know." I followed him out to the garden where guests were slowly departing and the staff clearing away the remains of the wake. Hudson approached Cecily while I hovered on the periphery. They were in earnest conversation and I overheard Cecily asking Hudson how on earth were they going to manage? It was then a thought came to me. Why could I not stay on an extra day or so to help them in their predicament? I went over and put my suggestion to Cecily.

"Oh, could you dear?" exclaimed Cecily the worry on her face now receding. "That would be marvelous and with your nursing experience why Charles would be in the best of care. Oh, it would be a weight off my mind. I am most grateful. If you need to use the telephone to contact anybody Hudson here will show you where it is."

I accompanied him to the telephone which was in an annex off the library and it was only a few minutes until the operator had connected me to the hospital. Matron was thank goodness understanding, advising me to come in when I was able. The next calls were to Audrey and Jean also empathic both hoping that I would not contract the virus and wishing me well. My calls completed I went again in search of Hudson to ask him about the acquisition of a bedpan or something similar for Charles. I located him in the library straightening the cushions on the sofa.

"Excuse me, Mr. Hudson, sorry to interrupt." He put the cushion down and stood to attention.

"Yes, madam."

"Well," I commented. "As Charles is to be confined to bed for some time I was wondering if you could possibly locate a bedpan or a commode?"

He looked rather flustered and had turned a shade of pink.

"Er, I seem to recall his lordship's father had the use of one when he was ill and it was put away in one of the storerooms. I will have the footman go and look for it right away."

"Thank you so much," I replied leaving him to his embarrassment and his cushions.

I ventured up the stairs to see how poor Charles was faring. Knocking softly on the door, I went in and found him awake but groggy.

"Hello, Charles, just thought I would pop in to see how you are." I walked over and stood by his bed. "In case you were not informed," I continued, "Mrs. Keen had to depart rather suddenly to take care of her sister. Apparently, she is suffering also from this wretched flu. Cecily was at her wits end so I took it upon myself to stay on a bit longer to nurse you if that's all right?"

He looked at me with eyes swollen with tears and managed to croak, "Oh, yes, that would be so good of you Peggy. Thank you, I'm so grateful, so sorry I am ill."

I said as brightly as I could, "Well, one never knows when the dreaded lurgy will strike." I glanced over at his bedside table and noticed the carafe of water was half full. "Now," I said, "make sure you drink lots of water. It will flush out the germs." I leaned over and felt his forehead. It seemed cooler than before, a good sign that his fever had broken although his pajamas appeared to be damp with sweat.

"I think you will need to change into some fresh pajamas."

"Oh, yes," he replied his nose sniffing one of the sleeves "these do seem to be rather unsavory. "There should be a clean pair in the second drawer of the chest in my dressing room." He waved his hand in the direction of the room. "I seem to remember that is where my valet used to keep them." He coughed again then sank down on the pillow. I walked over to the dressing room and rummaged in the second drawer of the chest. There were no pajamas there only multiple matching socks all expertly folded. I opened the third drawer which contained his night attire also folded neatly. I selected a smart pair of navy striped pajamas and brought them into him.

"Here we are, these look rather smart."

ଛଉଛଉଛଉ

I proceeded to divest him of the old pair and helped me on with the new. I then plumped up his pillows and gave him the tablets ensuring they were swallowed with a good amount of water. With a promise to check on him before I retired for the night I left his room and closed the door quietly.

Chapter Six

It was just Cecily, Bunny and I partaking of a light supper in the drawing room that evening. Apart from pea and ham soup, it was a cold collation of meats and salads all brought in by the footman. Considering the circumstances, I thought that was entirely appropriate to dispense with formalities. I would not have felt comfortable in the dining room at a table groaning with food with all the accoutrements of a formal setting. I was seated next to Bunny and wondered why he was still here. I thought he must be a very good friend of the family if he was also staying the night. To lighten the somber atmosphere a little I regaled him and Cecily with a couple of humorous anecdotes, one of which quite piqued his interest and sent him into paroxysms of laughter. It was not that funny, I mused. It was probably all the alcohol he had consumed at the wake and which he was continuing to consume. We adjourned to the library for a nightcap and a cigarette however it was not long until Cecily pleaded a headache and took herself to bed. I thought she had looked very peaky. It had been a terrible day for her losing her only daughter and her grandchild and I did feel most terribly sorry. Although she possessed a rather haughty attitude as had her daughter, my feelings towards her were warming and I did not have that sense of intimidation and condescension when Diana and I had first met.

I was feeling rather exhausted too. The day had been fraught with emotion. I finished my whiskey and extinguished my cigarette. I left Bunny to his port and cigar and made my way upstairs to check on Charles who I found to be sleeping. I checked his forehead which was thankfully cool then, ensuring there was enough water left in the carafe, quietly closed the door and went to my room.

It took me a while to fall asleep. There were so many thoughts jostling in my head. Here I was in this grand house, Hagley Hall, looking after Charles who was sleeping across the corridor from me. I thought of Diana and her baby now interred in the graveyard of the chapel. The internment had taken place after Charles had been taken ill, Cecily thinking that was the best course of action. He could pay his respects to them as soon as he felt well enough to cope. I thought about that Bunny fellow. What was his connection to the family? He certainly seemed to make himself at home, familiar with everyone, insinuating himself. I pulled up the covers and attempted to settle when there was a knock at the door. Who could that be I wondered, surely not Hudson or one of the maids at this hour? Surely Charles had not taken a turn for the worst. As I climbed from the bed the door suddenly was flung open and I was confronted by Bunny clad only in pajamas, a half bottle of port in his hand.

"Bunny, what are you doing here? "You should not be in my room. Please go back to bed."

However, he shut the door and pushing past me sat on the bed.

"Couldn't sleep," he said, "Thought we might finish our nightcaps here."

"I don't think that is a good idea, Bunny," I explained pulling my gown more tightly around me. "I have had a very tiring day and need to sleep now."

He pulled me down onto the bed "Oh go on, just a little tipple, it will help you relax," he said trying to force the drink into my mouth.

I pushed it away.

"Let me go, I don't want your drink, get out of here now," I shouted trying to extricate myself from him but had me pinned down. As I struggled he released his grip on the bottle which fell onto the floor rolling away and probably spilling its contents.

"Ok," he said, "There are other ways to relax. How about a bit of the old rumpy pumpy? Heard you nurses like a bit of that, what?" He said grabbing my breast.

"How dare you! Get your hands off me, get off!" I yelled, trying to push him away.

"Now calm down and give old Bunny a feel and a kiss." His leering face was inches from mine as he slobbered over me. As he forced his tongue between my lips the fumes of his alcoholic breath nearly made me retch and I could feel the hardness of his arousal. My God, I thought, am I going to be raped on the first night here in this house with Charles sleeping nearby? I would have to do something. I thought of my thick book on the table. "Bunny," I whispered in his ear, "I just have to use the facilities, let me up and then we can have some fun." He seemed to understand what I told him and after loosening his grip I managed to reach over and grab my book and with all the force I could muster hit him over the head with it. Stunned, he fell onto the floor.

"Bitch," he yelled as he pulled himself up and with whatever dignity he could garner slunk over to the door which I had now quickly opened. His parting words to me were that if I ever mentioned what had happened he would tell everyone it was I who had invited him in and they would believe him as he had been a family friend for years and I was just a blow in. He also told me I was probably a frigid bitch and not worth the trouble.

Shaking with the shock I ensured the door was locked. I sat on the bed nearly hysterical. How could he do such a thing? I did not give him any encouragement. I was not flirting with him. I was just being sociable. I looked over at the bottle which has spilled its contents on the floor. I went over and picked it up placing it on my bedside table. Doubtless, the maid will presume I am some sort of alcoholic when she sees the evidence in the morning when she has to clean the floor and dispose of the bottle. That is the least of my worries I thought as I returned to bed. How was I going to sleep now? As I lay looking at the cornice of the ceiling I determined I would not mention the episode to Charles. He had enough to worry about and I did not want to alienate him from his friend who might follow through with his plan to blackmail me. No, the best course of action was to keep quiet, try and put it to the back of my mind and try to avoid that Bunny as much as possible. I plumped my pillow, turned over and tried to think of happier things. However, sleep eluded me.

Chapter Seven

In the morning thoughts of the night before still rattled in my head. How was I going to confront them all, especially him? I hoped because of his drunkenness he might have forgotten what he had done. I heard some movement outside my door. It was probably the maid starting her day's work. There was a knock and I climbed out of bed to answer it.

"Good morning, madam, I'm Milly. Would you like me to draw a bath for you?" she asked.

"Oh, yes, that would be lovely."

I thought a long hot bath was just what I needed. It would help me relax before facing the fray downstairs. I donned my gown and putting up my hair made my way to the bathroom. Milly was putting out the towels which I noticed were monogrammed with the family crest. Beside the bath, there was a large cake of olive oil soap from Marseilles and a selection of French bath salts. I threw in a liberal quantity of those and stepped into the fragrant water. It felt so good and seemed to relax me steering my mind away from last night's disaster. I could have stayed there for hours but cognisant of the time and not wanting to be the last down for breakfast I dried off then hurried to my room to decide what I would wear. My selection was my tartan skirt and white blouse and I also decided to throw a red cardigan around my shoulders as I knew these grand houses could be rather chilly. I left my hair down and applied some lipstick then I left the room. I passed Milly in the corridor dusting the skirting boards and thought of her having to clean up the spilled port in my room. I was going to tell her but decided I had better not say anything. I surmised that maids must see all sorts of things in these houses and a little spilled drink and an empty bottle of port would be the least scandalous thing she had probably been witness to. She informed where I should go to have breakfast. I thanked her but decided I would first check on my patient. He was sitting up in bed with a tray on which resided a boiled egg and toast fingers.

"Good morning," I announced after knocking gently on the door. I walked over to the bed.

"How's the patient this morning? I'm glad to see you are eating something."

He looked at me and put his spoon down

"Oh, hello, yes I thought I would try a little food," he murmured desultorily dipping a toast soldier into the egg.

"I used to love egg and toast soldiers when I was little," I said brightly. As a matter of fact, I still do."

"Yes," he replied. "It is certainly comfort food. Nanny used to make it for me. It is just what one needs when one is feeling poorly. Have you had your breakfast?"

"No, I thought I would pop in first to see how you were."

"That was sweet of you," he wiped some egg from his mouth with the linen napkin. He was still pale and I noticed he was in need of a shave.

He continued after another fit of coughing, "But you must go and eat. There are usually kippers and eggs when we have only a few guests staying."

"That sounds delicious and a good deal better than the breakfast I usually have. Do you want me to bring you back anything after I have eaten?"

He placed his tray at the end of the bed.

"No, thank you. I don't require anything at the moment. I might have another nap."

Bequeathing him a smile I prepared to depart.

"Oh, wait," he called, "So sorry about this, but I think I need to use the lavatory. Hudson got this contraption out of storage. He pointed to the commode in the corner of the room.

"Of course," I replied, "I will help you over to it." I moved the tray off the bed and placing it on the floor helped him out of bed. Rather unsteadily he walked over with me to the commode and then sat down, albeit reluctantly.

"I will be just outside the door," I told him. "Let me know when you are ready to go back to bed."

"Jolly good, thanks. I must say this is quite embarrassing," I heard him say as I made my way to the door. I threw over my shoulder." Not at all Charles. I am used to dealing with far more than this in my occupation. Just take your time and let me know when to come in."

I waited a few minutes thinking about his discomfiture and then when I heard his signal went in to deal with the result of his efforts. I settled him into bed and told him I would return when the doctor arrived.

"Good morning madam," said Hudson as I entered the dining room.

"There are kippers and eggs in the chafing dishes," He went on. "It is a casual affair when we do not have many guests. Please help yourself. Would madam prefer tea or coffee?"

I sat down where a place was set with silver cutlery and a linen napkin.

"Tea. Thank you, Mr. Hudson."

"Where are the others this morning?" I enquired.

"I believe Lady Granville is taking breakfast in her room and Mr. Williams ate earlier. He was apparently taking the dogs for a walk and will be back later. Is his lordship any better today?" He asked.

"Yes, thank goodness. I just this minute looked in on him and he was trying some egg and toast. His fever has gone and he seems to be improving although his cough is still there. What time is the doctor due to call?"

"About eleven and he will be pleased his lordship is on the mend. Poor man, after all, he has suffered these past days, it is all too much for a body to bear, I must say." Shaking his head he went off to the kitchen to fetch the tea while I walked over to help myself to some kippers and poached eggs that were resting under domes of silver.

Thank heavens I am on my own this morning I thought as I sat down with my plate. I could not bear to be confronting that Bunny! He is making himself scarce, I hoped he would lose himself in the woods and never be found! I thought of Hudson mentioning that Cecily was Lady Granville then that would mean Diana had probably been a Lady also.

The measured tread of Hudson interrupted my thoughts as he returned with a pot of tea and a jug of milk. I was putting a kipper to my mouth when Cecily entered the room.

"Oh, there you are, my dear," she said pulling out a chair.

"So sorry I am not joining you for breakfast. I preferred to have it in my room this morning. I feel quite below par. Did you sleep well?"

"Not too bad, thank you," I lied. "I think everyone is feeling rather down at the moment."

Changing the subject, I said "By the way, Charles seems not too bad this morning. He was trying some egg and toast."

"That is good news," she replied her fingers worrying the beads at her neck.

"Thank you for helping us in our time of need, dear," she added.

I speared a kipper.

"Don't mention it. I am pleased I was able to be here."

"Have you seen Bunny this morning?" she then asked, the mention of his name sending a frisson of anxiety through me.

"He is such a great friend of Charles, you see," she continued, "I'm sure he would love to see him."

"Mr. Hudson told me he left early to take the dogs for a walk and would be back later," I replied.

"Oh, really? He does not usually go out this early when he stays. I suppose he will be back in good time for luncheon."

Hudson came in to enquire if Cecily required anything. She declined and said she would look in on Charles then getting off the chair she told me that luncheon would be served at twelve and would see me then if not before. She departed the room and as I swallowed the last mouthful of tea the maid entered to clear away the remnants of my meal.

Planning to visit Charles after the doctor had visited I decided to take a walk around the grounds as up until now there had been no time to see them properly. I went to my room to fetch my coat as I knew it would be still chilly then went downstairs. I opened the French doors and stepped through onto a beautiful terrace on which reclined a cast iron table and chairs surrounded by tubs spilling over with red and yellow hydrangeas and I envisaged dining there alfresco on a sunny summer day. Before me, there was a ha-ha and further out what looked like a maze. The place is like a castle I mused as I walked down the steps and across the grass still crunchy by the overnight frost. I walked towards the maze and, summoning courage, commenced walking through it hoping with every step I would find my way out and not have to call for someone to rescue me. Oh, God, to be trapped in here with that Bunny Williams! I started to panic and turned back the way I had come and thankfully found my way out. Looking over to the other side of the gardens I noticed a man clipping some shrubs. He must have been the gardener I saw from my window yesterday. I decided to walk over and introduce myself.

"Hello there," I said. He put down his secateurs and offered me his hand, a gardener's hand, rough, calloused.

"I'm Peggy Davis, a nurse and a friend of Lord Davenport," I explained.

"Ow do miss, pleased to meet you. How is his lordship? I heard he was poorly like."

"Yes, he is," I replied, "unfortunately he has influenza and the doctor advised him to stay in bed. I was invited to the funeral and offered to stay on for a couple of days to help look after him as the housekeeper had been called away."

"That was good of you, miss. His lordship has never had the best of health. I remember when he was a little chappie he was forever coming down with bad chests and now with her ladyship and the babbbie dead, God rest their souls." He said blessing himself, "It's a terrible to do, terrible." Clearly distressed, he wiped his eyes with a handkerchief that had seen better days.

"Yes," I replied, "It has been a very tragic time." I asked him, "Have you been here long, Mr...?"

"Mullins, miss, I'm Mr. Mullins and yes I have been here a good while. It will be nigh on forty years. I was took on when I were a lad by his lordship's father and been lookin' after these gardens ever since. I saw many changes down the years. Time was when this house was full of servants, but times have changed, what with that depression wot happened, but at least I still have a job and a roof over me head."

He was a lovely old man and was clearly enjoying a chat. I asked him,

"And is there a Mrs. Mullins?"

He blessed himself again as a cloud passed overhead putting us into shadow.

"No, God rest her soul. She passed away a few years ago. It is just me and Rastus now."

"Oh," I said. "I'm sorry about your wife, but who is Rastus?"

"He's me cat and he is a good age now and I think the way he is going he will outlive me and no mistake."

"Yes," I replied. "They do say cats have nine lives don't they?"

"They do, indeed."

I thought as he had been here for such a long time he might know something about Bunny Williams. I broached the subject.

"Mr. Mullins," I started, "there is a fellow called Bunny Williams staying here and I was wondering if you knew much about him?"

He looked around then leaning towards me said conspiratorily,

"Oh, him? I believe he has an interest in some cotton mills up Manchester way but his main interests lie in other directions."

"Oh," I replied my curiosity piqued.

"Yes," he continued "DWG."

"DWG? What's that?"

"Drinkin', women, and gamblin'." He smirked. "I don't know what his lordship sees in him, I don't, but they have been good friends for a long time. And, he continued, "I heard he was sent down from Oxford."

This Bunny fellow was becoming more intriguing by the minute and I was keen to learn a bit more.

"Why was that?" I asked.

"Well," he said still checking around to make sure no one was listening "It was something to do with a young lassie in his room, after hours, and I don't think he was teaching her the Latin if you know what I mean."

I certainly knew what he meant. This Bunny Williams certainly seemed to have a reputation.

Mullins looked at the sky.

"Well, I had better get on," he said, "those clouds over yonder look like they might have some rain in em'."

He bent down and picked up his secateurs.

"Goodbye then," I said, "I might see you around another day."

"Goodbye miss and give my regards to his lordship." Pointing his finger to his nose he added.

"And remember, mum's the word!"

Mum's the word indeed I thought. That Bunny was sounding quite a bounder and exploiting Charles' good nature at every opportunity. Leaving Mr. Mullins to his roses I walked on to one of the follies. The clouds were building so I quickened my steps and arrived just when the heavens opened. It was a white gothic style arrangement in which I sheltered and where I sat watching the rain tumble down. From my vantage point in the distance, I could see the great house rearing up in all its splendor. I thought if my sister could see me now sitting in this folly in the grounds of Hagley Hall, to say nothing of sleeping in one its rooms. I discerned the window of Charles' bedroom and wondered how he was and if the doctor had arrived. Then my thoughts turned to that Bunny character if he had returned from walking the dogs, how long he would stay and if he would depart after luncheon. I hoped he would but I supposed it did not really matter as I would soon be leaving anyway and hopefully would not lay eyes on him again. The rain abated and it was my opportunity to rush back to the house before another shower. Pulling up the collar of my coat I dashed back across the sodden grass.

"Hello, Mr. Hudson, "I said as I rushed through the door, "Is the doctor here yet?" I removed my coat from which a few spots of rain fell onto the marble floor.

"Yes, madam, the doctor is examining his lordship at this very minute." He bent down and with his handkerchief mopped up the moisture.

"Oh, good," I replied, "Then I shall go up and speak to him."

"Very well," he said his eyes traveling to my shoes which were noticeably wet. He, however, kept his counsel and closed the door. He purposefully strode away probably to check if the silver had been cleaned or to perform any other duties befitting a butler. I made my way to Charles' room just as the doctor was coming out. He reminded me of professor Newtown however he was not as tall or as supercilious.

"Hello, doctor. How is our patient this morning?"

"I am pleased to say his lordship is much improved," he replied "owing to the bed rest he has had. In my opinion, it is the best remedy as it gives the body time to heal. And, he added, "your nursing experience certainly helped."

I thanked him for his compliment and asked when Charles would be able to get up.

"Probably tomorrow, all being well and if he feels inclined there is no reason why he cannot come downstairs tonight for dinner."

I was pleased to hear that Charles was now on the mend and escorted the doctor downstairs leaving him in the capable hands of Hudson. I then returned to Charles' room.

"Well, that's good news," I said standing beside his bed. "The doctor just told me you might be able to get up later and come down to supper tonight."

"Oh, did he? Well, I will probably do that. One does tend to get bored when one is confined to one's room."

"Yes," I replied, "I hate to be ill too. One feels so useless."

He still looked rather wan and in need of a shave.

"What about I draw a bath for you?" I asked, "It will make you feel better."

His eyes brightened.

"That sounds jolly good although you do not have to do that. Milly should be available."

"No," I replied, "I am quite capable of running a bath. After all, I added, "It is part of my nursing duties."

I left him to put on his gown then went to the bathroom. Turning on the taps, I placed a cake of verbena soap on the side of the bath and a big fluffy towel on the chair. When I returned he was in his dressing room trying to find a pair of pajamas and some clean underwear.

"Ah," he announced, "Found them at last."

"I was about to select them for you," I told him "You are not the valet but the master and, the master's bath awaits." I smiled at him and noticed a detectable sign of a smile forming around his lips.

Smelling of Floris & Penhaligon toilet water, refreshed and shaved Charles was back in bed which had been freshly made by Milly while he was bathing. I was expecting her to give me a funny look as the memory of the spilled bottle of port still resided in my mind. However, her attitude had not changed, it had all been in her day's work and she had done a good job of cleaning the floor and disposing of the bottle. I noticed Charles was not coughing as much as previously and I could see he was trying to keep a stiff upper lip which was the want of an English gentleman.

"I hope you feel better now Charles," I said straightening the cover. "Would you like Milly to bring you up something to eat? Mr. Hudson said luncheon is to be served at twelve and it is nearly that time. I suppose I should make an appearance."

"Yes, you had better go down. See if they can rustle up some soup if you don't mind."

"Alright, I shall let the kitchen know. I'm so glad your appetite is returning. I shall pop in again after luncheon. Bon appétit, Charles."

కాకాకా

Closing the door I went downstairs with his order then made my way into the dining room. Cecily already seated at the table was addressing Hudson. "I don't know where he could have got to. He has been away with the dogs since early this morning. It is really quite improper being so unpunctual and having everyone waiting for their luncheon. I think Hudson, you had better serve us and he will just have to eat whenever he returns."

"Very good, your Ladyship," answered Hudson pulling out a chair for me. He added as he went through to the kitchen. "I do hope nothing has befallen Mr. Williams."

Cecily turned towards me. "Oh, Peggy. So sorry to have not greeted you but I am concerned about Bunny Williams."

"Yes," I replied meeting her gaze "I gather he has not made an appearance." To allay her concern I suggested the dogs may have run off and he was trying to locate them.

Hudson brought in the potato and leek soup followed by a spinach and mushroom roulade. I was feeling rather peckish as I had been unable to finish my breakfast and the walk I had taken must have given me an appetite. Over the soup, Cecily asked about my morning, what I had been up to. I told her about my walk around the grounds, my meeting with Mr. Mullins and my unsuccessful foray into the maze. This brought a smile to her face as she recounted her experience with Diana when they had first attempted to walk through. It had been their shouts and yells which had brought one of the footmen to their rescue. I was pleased that she felt able to talk about her daughter without becoming distressed. She had commented on Mr. Mullins, how long he had been here and that Charles was fortunate in having such a faithful retainer. We conversed about Charles' illness and his recovery and the good news he might be joining us for dinner. As Hudson was placing the cheese and fruit on the table we were startled by a ruckus in the hall. "What the devil?" exclaimed Hudson. He hurried over to the door to ascertain the source of the noise and was nearly bowled over by two dogs and Bunny Williams clearly inebriated staggering behind them.

"Where's my lunch old sport?" he shouted at Hudson who exhibited a complete look of disdain for the unruly guest disrupting the sanctity of the dining room.

"Or don't you wait for your bloody guests anymore?" he again shouted knocking over a chair and sending the dogs into a frenzy. They skidded across the floor and pelted out the door in a cacophony of barking. Cecily clearly shocked and disgusted exchanged glances with me. Bunny was quite inebriated and I suspected had been drinking for most of the morning. What else he had been up to I would not care to contemplate.

Drawing himself up to his full height, Hudson came over to Bunny who was holding on to the table in an effort to steady himself.

"Now, sir, that language is quite inappropriate in front of the ladies," he said trying to grab Bunny's elbow to escort him out of the room.

"Leave me alone," he yelled. "I don't see any ladies here. Maybe one," he added pointing crookedly at Cecily who now held a napkin to her face trying to avert her eyes from the unfolding spectacle.

"Come along to your room sir and have a lie down." Hudson managed to steer him out of the room leaving a trail of expletives in his wake.

We sat there in disbelief and shock at what had just transpired. Cecily wiping her mouth with her napkin pushed back her chair, stood up and apologized that I had to witness such uncouth and abominable behavior. She said she was returning to her room where she would spend the rest of the afternoon and would see me tonight at dinner. I wished her well and then I too departed. En route to my room, I thought about Bunny Williams and if I should tell Charles but, according to Mr. Mullins' account, it was obviously par for the course.

As the rain had cleared and I did not relish the thought of being confined to my quarters I decided to take a walk into the village. After informing Charles who was sitting in bed enjoying a book, I grabbed my coat and bag and set off. A good walk would be just what I needed. It would help me gather my thoughts and clear my head. Although the grass was still wet it was not a concern as I had put on some sturdy walking shoes. I walked past the gazebo in which I had sheltered this morning and then on to the private driveway along which Bill had driven me a few days ago. I could not believe it had only been that long as with all that had transpired, it had seemed a lot longer. I breathed in the crisp air scented with the rain-soaked earth, the cry of a wren the only sound.

Setting a good pace, it was not long before I reached the road leading to the village. As I approached, I noticed there were a few people about. It looked a charming little place; a general store selling all kinds of requirements, a quaint tea shop and a pub called The White Hart where undoubtedly Bunny Williams had overly imbibed. There was a bright red letterbox and dominating all was the steeple of an ancient church which looked as though it had grown out of the earth millennia ago. I pushed open the heavy wooden door and entered. It was quite dark inside and had the smell which old churches all seemed to possess, cold stale air and candle wax. I walked over to where some candles flickered and lit one. I knelt down on the kneeler, closed my eyes and prayed. Firstly, for my mother and the child I lost and for Diana and her baby. I asked God to help me forgive my father for his transgressions imposed on me. I asked God to restore Charles to good health, to give him the strength to cope with his loss and again have happiness in his life. I wanted to be part of that happiness. I felt I was being drawn to him, that there had been some connection the first time we had our encounter in Harrods. But then I thought it was obviously propinquity, two people thrown together as I cared for him in his hour of need. It was quite silly to think anything of a romantic nature would occur. He had just lost his wife and baby! I opened my eyes to shafts of sunlight which were illuminating the stained-glass window above the altar. To my amazement, I noticed the window contained similar biblical scenes as the ones featured in the chapel at Hagley Hall. Was this some sort of portent I wondered as I blessed myself and walked back out into bright sunshine?

The teashop beckoned. I located a table near the window where I sat watching the passing parade of people, the fine weather having enticed them all outside.

As I sipped my tea and nibbled the poppy seed cake which I ordered I wondered about tonight. Would Charles feel well enough to join us for dinner, would I be seated near him and not near Bunny Williams who I hoped had by now sobered up and was chastened? I sat there until the light was commencing to fade then after paying the bill I retraced my steps back to Hagley Hall where I came across Hudson with Bill who was polishing the car.

"Good afternoon, madam."

"Hello, Mr. Hudson, hello Bill," I replied.

Bill looked up and doffed his cap.

"Have you been walking?" asked Hudson.

"Yes, I took myself into the village."

"Very good madam," Hudson said. "I am glad the weather fined up for you and you had a pleasant time."

"Yes, I did very much." I looked across at Bill.

"Excuse me, Bill," I said, "I am sorry to interrupt but I was thinking of going home tomorrow. If it is not too much trouble, I wonder if you could please drive me to the station?"

"Certainly miss. What train were you thinking of taking?"

"I'm not sure at the moment," I replied "Charles may know how often the trains run as he told me what train to catch when I came here. I shall ask him and let you know a bit later if that is alright."

He agreed to my plan and then continued on with his polishing as Hudson stood by pointing out to him the spots he had overlooked.

I walked through to the library where I discovered Cecily leafing through an old copy of The Tatler. She beckoned me over to have a word.

"Hello, Peggy, dear," she said motioning me to sit down on the sofa beside her.

"I'm so sorry for that ruckus at luncheon. I hope it did not upset you too much. I will have to have a word with Charles when things are back to normal. I had to spend the afternoon in my room to recover."

I met her gaze and put my hand on hers.

"I know," I agreed, "it was not very pleasant was it?"

"What did you do with yourself," she asked.

"I took a walk into the village."

"Oh, that was a nice thing to do." She replied.

"And did you go into that old church while you were there?"

"Yes, as a matter of fact, I did."

"It is Saxon," she explained, "and has the same windows as the ones here at the Hall."

She went on to say that many years ago the church was part of the estate and when the Hall was built the chapel windows were built in a similar design.

The house had such history I mused as my eyes roamed the room. They alighted on shelves of books probably among them first editions, their gilded spines glowing in the light from the lamps. There was a portrait of King George V1 hanging over the fireplace and an inlaid desk sat between the bookshelves on the far wall. It was only now I felt able to really appreciate this library. Last night I had been enveloped in melancholy, trying to make conversation with strangers.

"Yes," said Cecily bringing me back to the discussion. "It is certainly a grand house. It has been in Charles' family for centuries."

"Well," I said, "I am certainly going to miss it as I plan to go home tomorrow."

"Oh, tomorrow, are you dear? Well, I am sure we will all miss you. You have been a godsend to us. But, of course, you have your life to lead in London and your patients must be awaiting your return."

I told her Bill had kindly offered to drive me to the station.

"I will ask Charles about the train times," she said adding that she hoped he could join us for supper as she felt sorry for him cooped up in his sickroom.

I wondered about Cecily. When she planned to go home and where was her home?

"Do you know when you are returning home, and where might that be?" I ventured.

"I have an apartment in Belgrave Square where I have lived for many years. It was where Diana grew up." At the mention of her name tears welled in her eyes and she brushed them away. She continued, "I will probably stay on for a few more days or at least until Mrs. Keen comes back and Charles has fully recovered. I dare say my maid will be tiring of looking after my little pooch and I do not want to outstay my welcome here although it has been mutually comforting for Charles and me in our time of grief."

"Well, I do hope you have happier days in the future, Cecily and what is it they say? Time heals all wounds."

"Thank you, dear and I do hope that will be the case. Now, dinner is at eight and we will meet in the drawing room for drinks around sevenish."

I left her to her magazine and went to see the patient. On the way, I wondered about Cecily's husband, who he was and if he was still alive. I had not wanted to ask her in the library. I thought it would be inappropriate so soon after her daughter's death.

∞∞∞

I found Charles up and dressed, looking and sounding so much better. There was more color to his cheeks and the circles under his eyes had almost disappeared. However, when I had told him of my departure plans his face fell momentarily then recovering his composure he said he had something to ask me. I wondered what it was. He motioned me over to the chaise.

"Peggy," he commenced.

What on earth was he going to say?

"I was wondering if before you go you would accompany me to the graveyard. You see I have not paid my respects yet."

"Oh, oh, but of course, certainly," I gushed, "It would be my pleasure." So that was what he had to ask. I was relieved it was that request, it was what I could handle. I had wondered when he was going to make the pilgrimage. It had probably been uppermost in his mind as he lay in his sickbed.

As though a weight had been lifted his mood brightened,

"Thank you," he said taking my hand as his eyes met mine.

We arose from the couch.

"Well I suppose I will see you later," he said as he walked me to the door.

"Yes," I replied with a smile "In the drawing room around seven."

I went straight to my room to select something appropriate to wear. As I dragged a few dresses off the hangers, I thought tonight I would see Charles in a social setting. I selected a black dress that fit me like a glove. I spent time freshening up in the bathroom and more time expertly applying my makeup. I tried reading my book but found my concentration lacking, all my thoughts were concentrated on tonight. It was a quarter to seven when I decided to put my hair into a chignon as I knew it enhanced my cheekbones. Stepping into my black strappy shoes which I had fortunately packed, I placed the strand of pearls around my neck. Then, with a final dab of perfume behind my ears and my wrist, I was ready for the night and whatever it would bring.

Bunny Williams was draped across the chaise-longue as I entered the room. Smoking a Turkish cigarette and with a glass, in hand he beckoned me over. I ignored him and was rescued by the footman offering me a glass of champagne. As I was feeling the bubbles hitting my nose Charles walked in. He was wearing a grey smoking jacket and looked quite debonair. He approached and ushered me over to the sofa on the other side of the room opposite Bunny.

I could feel Bunny's eyes on me, scrutinizing, assessing. I was wishing he would make a fool of himself in front of Charles just as he had at the luncheon. I took a good swallow of champagne to ease my nerves and focused my attention on Charles. Cecily then came in. Dressed in an emerald green dress she looked rather youthful, the color setting off the highlights in her hair which was the same color as Diana's had been. I visualized what color the baby's might have been, whether it would have been auburn like her mother or dark brown like Charles.

Bunny sidled over.

"Hello Bunny, said Charles. "Have you been amusing yourself while I have been laid low?"

"Never worry about old Bunny, sport," he replied blowing a curl of smoke into the air. He then proceeded to plonk himself right next to me. I could feel his eyes taking in my legs and I shifted a bit towards Charles.

"Always something around here to keep a chap entertained."

Charles took a drink from the passing footman.

He looked over at Bunny and enquired.

"When were you thinking about going back to Manchester? There must be things needing attention. Cotton mills cannot run on their own for long."

"Everything's in hand, old chum." He took another swig of his drink. I thought it was astonishing how much alcohol he could put away in one day.

"As a matter of fact," he continued, "I'm motoring down to London tomorrow, meeting up with a couple of chums from the old alma mater. Thought we might take in the Goodwood Cup. Heard there is a dead cert in race seven, don't you know? Old Bunny could do with winning a few quid." He gushed.

Charles immediately interjected.

"What a coincidence. Peggy has decided to leave for London tomorrow. You could give her a lift. She was catching the train. What good luck, Peggy."

I was flabbergasted! There was no way I would ever contemplate going anywhere with him, much less driving to London. Apart from anything else, he would probably lose whatever money he put on his dead cert and come running to Charles to bail him out.

"Oh, er, thank you," I stammered. "But actually I rather enjoy traveling by train looking at the scenery and relaxing. And, I don't like to impose on anyone."

With a salacious look, Bunny turned to me.

"No imposition at all. Always like a pretty girl with me in the two-seater with the wind in her hair, just the ticket, what?" He got up from the sofa and throwing over his shoulder,

"Plenty of room in the dickey for luggage and such." He sauntered over and helped himself to olives and another glass of champagne which the footmen had placed on one of the tables.

He really was insufferable. I would have to think of something to head him off. I was in need of a gasper. Rummaging in my bag I discovered I had left the cigarettes in my room.

"Charles, I seem to have left my cigarettes in my room. Would you have one?"

"Certainly, and I also have a light." He offered me a cigarette from his case and then expertly lit it with an expensive-looking gold lighter.

"Thank you," I said as I inhaled. The cigarette and the champagne had the desired effect. I felt myself relax and was unperturbed about Bunny Williams who had now buttonholed the footman probably coercing him into giving him another drink.

I turned to Charles and was thankful that he had not decided to smoke. He was obviously cognizant of the fact that he was still recovering from his illness. I said as much,

"You are being sensible refraining from smoking."

"Oh, well, actually I don't know about sensible," he replied, "it's just that my taste buds seem to be rather all awry and I don't really feel like indulging."

"Is my smoking bothering you?" I asked.

"No, it isn't."

He sipped his drink. He seemed to be in a contemplative mood.

He turned to me and asked.

"Because you and I have been on close terms here the last few days I suppose I had better ask you a little about yourself."

I leaned over and ashed my cigarette in the tray which had been placed there by the footman.

"Ah," I said as I met his gaze, "My life story. Well, I'm afraid there is not much to tell. I grew up in Sussex, in Arundel. I have a sister, Rachel. Our father was the local solicitor. We attended a Catholic school and I did my training at St Margaret's Hospital in London where I am now, and, I added "I was married for a short time. My husband died a few years ago."

"Oh, I am sorry, and your parents, are they still alive?"

"No, unfortunately, they are both deceased. I was very close to my mother and miss her very much."

He reached over and patted my hand. It was a simple gesture but one which seemed full of empathy. I was unsure of his reaction when I told him I had been married but was pleased he did not want me to elaborate. I was always trying to put the memories of my marriage to the back of my mind but they had a habit of worming their way through when I least expected.

He asked about my sister, the difference in ages. I told him that she was three years older than me. Then, after more champagne, my tongue became loose and I found myself moving closer to him and confiding in him and telling him about my relationship with my sister. How we were not close, how she was consumed with jealousy of me, how she would belittle me at every opportunity making me feel inadequate and not as intelligent as she. The words came tumbling out.

"I am sorry to hear that Peggy," he replied, "Sibling rivalry can be trying or so I have heard. Fortunately, I have not experienced it as I was the only child, although there were times when I would have liked to have had a brother for company." He smiled and as an afterthought said, "Maybe I would have been the one to foist my wrath and jealousy on him." I could not imagine that he had a jealous bone in his body or would exhibit any kind of wrath.

He was about to say something else and I had sensed it may have been something confidential but then Cecily approached.

"Charles," she said, "Are you aware that Peggy is leaving us tomorrow?"

"Yes, I know." He said as he turned towards me "And we will certainly miss her smiling face."

Then, "Perhaps you should come and stay another time. As you know there is no shortage of beds."

"Oh," I replied, "I would love to."

"Then that's settled." He put down his glass and rose from the sofa then proffered his hand to assist me.

"Now," he said, "I think it is time for Hudson to announce dinner."

As I walked with Charles towards the dining room I asked him what was Bunny Williams' correct name and why was he called Bunny? It was a simple explanation. He had been a crack shot at shooting rabbits and had never missed one. Thence the name had stuck. I thought I could think of lots of names for him and they would not be as nice as the one he had been labeled with.

We took our seats at the table which was replete with gleaming crystal glasses and Limoge dinnerware. Candles flickered from candelabra and vases of flowers were placed at intervals along the table. The room had been transformed. It did not resemble the room in which I had breakfast the morning after my traumatic encounter with Bunny Williams. That morning I had been in too great a state to take in the magnificence of this room. My eyes had not traveled to the paintings in their heavy gilt frames adorning the walls, the Renoirs and Monets as well as pastoral scenes. Nor had I noticed the swathes of scarlet velvet curtains at the windows and the Persian rugs scattered over the floor.

My attention was diverted by the footman who was bringing in the first course, a consommé. Charles was seated on my right, Bunny opposite and Cecily on my left. Initially, the conversation was desultory. It was over the poached salmon and rack of lamb that the subject turned to the German situation, what I had gleaned from the newspaper. Bunny had exclaimed that if there was another war he would look forward to putting a few bullets up those German arses. That statement had Cecily putting her hand over her mouth, quite disgusted with his language. I, however, was not easily shocked as I heard worse than that every day in the wards of St Margaret's. The footman kept replenishing our glasses until I put my hand over mine signaling I did not require any more. After all the champagne I had drunk previously I did not wish to disgrace myself as Bunny had. I stole a glance at him downing another glass, his voice rising a few decibels the more he drank. He saw me watching him. He stabbed a piece of lamb with his fork and with eyes narrowed leaned towards me reminding me of our journey tomorrow, of how long it would take and his intention to call in at one of the inns for a snifter. I ignored him and was in disbelief that after being thrown out of my room he was still trying his luck. There was no stopping him. He was incorrigible. I turned my attention to Charles who was telling Cecily he was considering selling a few acres to the colonel who lived on the other side of the valley and had scheduled a meeting with him tomorrow. He spoke of his intention to call in on one of his tenant farmers during the week to discuss the renewal of his tenancy. Cecily asked him if he intended to have someone look at the problem of the dry rot in the roof which apparently was an ongoing concern. I absorbed it all, how big this estate was and how much work was involved in maintaining it. Up until now, I had not realized. I had thought people like Charles spent their time dining on fine food at a grand table or ensconced beside a fire, brandy in hand after a stroll around the grounds. Now I knew it was far from that. The footman brought a Queen of Puddings dessert and there was a break in the conversation. It would be my opportunity to ask Charles about the train timetable as there was no way I would be traveling with that leering drunk opposite.

"Charles," I whispered. "I really do not fancy driving to London with Bunny tomorrow, by the look of him I don't think he would not be in a fit state."

He agreed then asked what time I would prefer to leave.

"I thought around nine. It would give me time after we have been to the cemetery."

At the mention of the cemetery, his face became cloaked with sadness and I had wished I had not spoken, however it had been his idea to go with me before I left. But then it was understandable he would feel upset as his feelings were still raw and obviously there would be more occasions when a mention of a word or a name would conjure up sadness.

He then assumed a business-like manner, pushed back his chair and said to me," I will go and let Bill know before he retires,"

"Where's he gone?" snarled Bunny swiveling his head towards Charles' retreating back.

"Aren't we bloody good enough for him anymore?" He stood unsteadily and knocked over the glass of claret spilling the contents and turning the tablecloth a bright shade of pink, which matched the tones of Cecily's face.

The footman rushed over to mop up the spill with Hudson following close behind. He took hold of Bunny's arm and with much protestation Bunny was escorted out to the library where Hudson endeavored to ply him with coffee in an effort to sober him up. Hudson must be so tired of him I thought, having always to escort him to other quarters in his inebriated states but being the efficient servant that he was he seemed to take it all in his stride.

Cecily came over and again apologized for Bunny's shocking conduct. She also opined that Charles should have a word in his ear. "The cheek of that man, he is a guest here after all. He really takes advantage of Charles. He is a disgrace." With that, she bade me good night as she had had enough shocks for one day, then retreated to her room saying she would see me tomorrow before I left. Charles returned with the news that Bill had been seconded to drive me to the station in plenty of time to catch the train. He inquired if I would like coffee in the library but I declined his offer as I did not want to encounter Bunny and told him so.

"We could take some in the drawing room if you like. I can ask Hudson to rustle up some."

"No, thank you, Charles," I said, "If you don't mind, I think I shall retire." I had to pack my clothes and I wanted to awake early as I had something planned.

"Thank you for a beautiful night," I told him "I shall always remember it."

As I descended into a dreamless sleep my final thought was of my hand in his and that kiss he had lightly placed on my cheek.

Chapter Eight

"Sleeping together in the arms of God" read the inscription on the headstone and on the grave lay a posy of flowers with a tiny card attached. I thought Cecily or one of the servants had placed it there and was about to ask Charles when suddenly he became angry. He grabbed it off the grave and hurled it away. I did not know what to think or do. Why was he so angry about a bunch of flowers? I gave him the roses I had picked as icy rain commenced to fall. He composed himself and placed them on the grave. I did not tell him how I crept down the stairs before dawn hoping that the maids would not see me as they were always up early, cleaning out the grates, lighting the fires and preparing the breakfast.

"Thank you for bringing the roses and for coming," whispered Charles. He had composed himself now, his anger had abated. "I don't think I could have done this on my own."

"Charles," I said taking his cold hand. I wanted to warm it, rub it in mine.

"I was glad I was able to be with you. One needs support when tragedy strikes. Now, let's say a prayer." We bowed our heads and sent our personal messages and then were aware of someone approaching across the grass. It was Hudson armed with huge umbrellas.

"Your lordship, madam," he cried, "Get yourselves under these. You will catch your deaths out here, oh, beg pardon I did not mean to say that, quite inappropriate," he mumbled.

I felt sorry for poor Hudson, for his slip of the tongue talking of death in the precinct of the graveyard as we put ourselves under the umbrellas. A vision in black, he hurried on ahead of us to attend to his duties.

We walked in silence for a while until Charles conveyed his appreciation for the roses which had been Diana's favorite flower. He had been more appreciative when I had told him of my surreptitious venture stealing out from the house at dawn and into the garden with my trusty nail scissors. I did not tell him of the thorns which had pricked my fingers nor the cold which seeped into my bones and I did not enquire about that posy which he had hurled from the grave causing him such anger.

Upon arrival at the house, Hudson was back on duty taking our sodden umbrellas as we came in the door.

"I have taken the liberty, madam," he said, "of having your suitcase collected from your room. Bill has placed it in the car so there will no delay in your drive to the station."

"Thank you so much, Mr. Hudson," I replied, "That was very kind of you." I asked, "Is Cecily around? I must say goodbye to her before I go."

Said Charles, "I will locate her Peggy, you go up and bring down anything else you may have left in your room."

I did as he suggested and went upstairs. I took the opportunity of using the lavatory and checking my appearance in the mirror. There was a glow to my cheeks from the bracing air and I only needed a reapplication of lipstick and a stray tendril tucked behind my ear. After a glance around my room, I took my handbag off the bed. Would I again sleep here I wondered or was Charles' invitation to stay just a politeness? I closed the door.

When I came downstairs Cecily was in the foyer with her arms outstretched.

"Goodbye, Peggy dear," as she enfolded me in a hug. "Thank you so much for your help in all our travails. Do have a safe journey home and hopefully we will see you again in the not too distant future." She turned towards Charles.

"Now, Charles, I hope you are going with Bill to see Peggy off?"

"Of course, I would not dream of abandoning our guest on a deserted station in the cold and rain."

Bill drove up to the entrance and Hudson with another umbrella ushered us into the car.

To frantic waves, we drove off along the beech-lined drive and on through the iron gates, the same journey I had taken only a few days before. It had seemed longer than that, so much had happened since then. I glanced over at Charles who was looking through the window. He seemed preoccupied. What were his thoughts? Was he thinking of his dead wife and child, that mysterious posy of flowers he had thrown, the meeting he was having with the colonel or the dry rot which had to be eliminated? Maybe he was thinking about Bunny, how he was going to address his behavior. I was sure if I apprised him of how he had acted towards me that night he would surely have to accost him. Our silence was companionable, not uncomfortable. We seemed to share an understanding, an acceptance that one does not have to constantly communicate. I was quite content just to have my hand patted occasionally and to receive a smile.

We had arrived at the station. Bill alighted. He took an umbrella and my suitcase from the boot and signaled a porter who hurried over to transport the bag to the luggage room.

"Thank you, Bill," said Charles as Bill opened the door. Charles stepped out and took the open umbrella then helped me from the car.

"Wait here for me." Commanded Charles.

The platform was deserted and due to the rain assumed a melancholic facade. It seemed to match how I was feeling, leaving Charles and Hagley Hall with all its splendor and memories good and bad.

Charles grasped my hand. He looked at me the way he had looked at me when he had lit my cigarette.

"Thank you so much for everything," he gushed. "I really don't know how we or I could have managed without you, without your compassion and your kindness."

I went to reply but was drowned out by the noise of the train as in a cloud of steam it roared into the station. I waited until the noise had subsided but before I had a chance to speak Charles said, "I wonder if you are free the week after next, would you like to have dinner with me as a token of my gratitude? I will be in London on business and will be staying in my apartment in Knightsbridge."

"All aboard!" cried the guard.

"Oh," I exclaimed as the train hissed its impatience to depart, "Why yes. I would love to, thank you."

He helped me up the steps as I felt his lips on my cheek.

I located my compartment then hurried to the window. Through it, I could see him mouthing the words that he would write to me as the train pulled away from the station.

I smiled and waved vigorously until I lost sight of him then settled in my seat for the journey home. I took my book from my bag and tried to read but my mind kept returning to Charles. He had looked so forlorn standing on that deserted platform in the rain and I wished I could have put my arms around him to give him solace. However, I contented myself that there had been hope in his eyes when I had accepted his invitation to dinner and

I had discerned a detectable smile lighting his face. He had paid for this first-class compartment in which I was ensconced waving away my protestations saying it was the least he could do for all the assistance I had rendered. I was sharing the compartment with a couple of businessmen doubtless going to London for a meeting and there was a smartly dressed woman in a cloche hat poring over a crossword. It was all very civilized and congenial not like what I had to endure on the way to Millbrook with that rambunctious woman spilling tea on my skirt.

Through the window, the landscape was wreathed in mist and rain. Bedraggled sheep huddled together under whatever shelter they could find to escape the elements. It was so different to the day I had journeyed up here when everything had been bathed in sunlight. I thought of Bunny Williams if he was still in bed with a hangover and then waking to find his traveling companion had absconded. I took my book from my bag and commenced reading and it seemed no time until the familiar chimney pots and grey drabness signaled the outskirts of London.

Euston was as busy as ever and although the rain had ceased the streets were sodden and slippery. I managed to attract a cab and scrambled in. Arriving home after being caught in heavy traffic it was good to be indoors at last. I carried my suitcase upstairs then thought about what there was to eat in the house. Rummaging through the cupboard all I could locate were some cans of baked beans. I would have to purchase some essentials to tide me over. Fortunately, the local shops were a stone's throw away so with my purse, basket and umbrella I set off. My umbrella was tiny compared to the ones Hudson had used I mused as I walked along. Hudson. Charles' faithful servant, I wondered what he would be doing now. Was he admonishing one of the staff for not polishing the silver to his standards or counting the number of wine bottles ensuring none had been pilfered? I arrived at the shop and after buying some eggs, bread and cheese hurried home with my purchases. I lit the fire and put the kettle on to boil then sorted through the mail which had piled up in my absence. As I sat beside the fire enjoying a cheese sandwich and a cup of tea I thought about going back to work tomorrow. It would be good to see my friends and colleagues and immerse myself in the activities of the wards and it would take my mind of Hagley Hall and all its memories.

Finishing my snack I turned my attention to the mail. Amongst the usual bills and flyers, there was a letter from the Post Office notifying me if I required the connection of the telephone. It certainly would be convenient having one in the house instead of having to walk down the street in all weather and also Charles could ring me instead of writing.

The queue in the post office was light as it was late afternoon and most people had conducted their business. A helpful lady served me and handed me a form to complete which I was able to do on the spot and she advised that a technician would come to my flat next

Wednesday. That day was perfect as Wednesday was usually my day off. After purchasing some stamps I made my way out. The wind was now up and I was trying to stop my umbrella blowing inside out as were many other of my fellow pedestrians. Passing the butcher I noticed some lamb chops in the window so I decided to buy a couple. They would go with the one potato I had spied sulking in the pantry and would suffice for my dinner. It would certainly be different from what I had consumed in Hagley Hall. In the buffeting wind, I headed home anxious to be inside where I knew the fire would be welcoming.

Chapter Nine

"Nurse Davis, you are back," exclaimed matron as I presented myself for duty. "I hope everything went as well as could be expected in Bedfordshire?"

"Yes, thank you, matron. It was certainly a very tragic time for everyone. I appreciated your permission to be absent for a few days."

"Very good." She scanned a page of admissions.

"Now, there is a prima gravida, a potential breach in ward nine, so please go there and make yourself useful."

"Of course, right away matron,"

As I scooted along the corridor thinking she was still the same officious person I encountered one of my favorite porters. He had been with the hospital for many years and was due for retirement.

"Hello, Mike, another busy day for you?" I asked him as he was in the process of wheeling an obese patient on a gurney from the operating suite.

"Oh hello, Peggy," he replied. "Yes, it looks like it will be one of those days. I haven't stopped since I started at

4.30 this morning." I walked along beside him as he huffed and puffed thinking the sooner he retires the better he will feel.

He looked over.

"Audrey was telling me you have been in the country."

"Yes, I went to help a friend who had a death in the family but now I am back on deck. I must track her down as I have lots to tell her."

"Well, it does a body good to see your smiling face around here again, and no mistake."

And then he was gone, lost in the labyrinth of the wards.

I hurried on toward ward nine as matron had instructed and there encountered professor Newton and an anesthesiologist administering chloroform to the prima gravida whose feet were in the stirrups. When she was adequately sedated the professor's skills were summoned to deliver a baby who was lying in the breech position. I stood by to assist in whatever capacity I could. I knew it would be a difficult birth as the baby was presenting bottom first instead of a normal head presentation. I watched as the professor applied pressure on the mother's abdomen using the external cephalic version to try to turn the baby, but it was unsuccessful. However, when the next strong contraction came, he was able to twist the baby's body so that an arm trailed behind the shoulder and crossed down over its face to a position where the professor's finger could reach. Then the same procedure was enacted on the opposite side, and with the use of the forceps, the baby was born without any mishap. I felt great admiration for the professor, as, for all his pomposity, he certainly had dealt with a very serious situation with great skill and professionalism.

The afterbirth was left for me to deal with and after cleaning mother and child a seven pounds six healthy boy, I swaddled and placed him in a crib to be transported to the nursery. On my way there I again met Mike talking to one of the cleaners.

"Hello, again Peggy, Jean, and Audrey were looking for you. They said they would be in the tearoom in about half an hour."

"Oh, right. Thanks, Mike." Resuming my trek to the nursery with my precious charge I left Mike to his conversation with the cleaner who appeared to be receiving rather a tongue lashing. It again put me in mind of Mr. Hudson.

Placing the infant's crib alongside his howling neighbors I left the baby in the competent hands of the nursery sister. I wished her a good afternoon but from the pandemonium, I was quite sure it would be far from good. After taking a few temperatures and checking the charts I made tracks for the tea room. It was full of the usual chattering nurses, cigarettes and tea in hand enjoying their break. Amongst the fray, I spotted Jean pouring her tea from the urn. I tapped her on the shoulder.

"Oh, Peg, here you are at last," she cried putting down her cup and giving me a hug. "It's so good to see you. Aud is over there by the window." I looked over and waved then helped myself to some tea which had not improved in my absence. Jean and I walked over to Audrey who had managed to purloin a couple of chairs before anyone had a chance to grab them.

"How did everything go?" asked Jean leaning towards me.

"Yes," chimed in Audrey "we are bursting to know all your news."

I took a good swallow of tea liberally laced with sugar. My energy level at the moment seemed to require a boost. Then I related my news. I told them how I was collected at the station by Bill, the chauffeur and being driven through the huge iron gates to the splendor of Hagley Hall. I told them about dear Mr. Hudson, the butler, the footman, Milly the maid and the poignancy of the funeral.

"Yes, but what about Charles?" Audrey wanted to know. Jean nodded in agreement.

"Oh, yes, well, of course, it was a terrible ordeal for him and the influenza did not make matters any better," I replied.

I could tell they wanted more details about Charles but I felt disinclined to tell them. I wanted to keep them to myself for a while. However, I told them about Bunny Williams, his drunkenness, how he ingratiated himself there and took advantage of Charles. I did not tell them of his attempt to rape me in my bed. That would keep for another day. My friends found amusing the story of his disappearance that morning to reappear drunk and cursing with the dogs going berserk.

"He sounds rather a character," said Jean putting her cup down on the table.

"That would be an understatement," I replied.

"And how was Charles when you left?" asked Jean "Had he recovered from his illness?"

"I think he is now on the road to recovery. And," I added, "he has actually invited me to dinner in a few weeks to show his gratitude for my assistance."

Their eyebrows rose.

"What? And are you going?" exclaimed Audrey her eyes aglow.

I looked down at my cup and then looked at my friends.

"Yes, I told him I would."

"Well, it gets better and better," said Jean. "I wonder where he will take you."

"Probably to some swanky place like the Ritz," Put in Audrey.

I had thought that was where he might take me. It would certainly not be one of the local pubs. Maybe we might go to a private club. I had heard of a few which catered for the gentry and people of Charles' ilk.

Audrey consulted her watch.

"Well, looks like we will have to curtail this little gossip session and return to it another time." Cutting me a look she said, "It will be hard for you to settle down Peg after all that luxury with servants at your beck and call."

"To say nothing of your upcoming dinner engagement with the lord of the manor," chortled Jean.

We stood up and took our cups over to the table and agreed to meet on Thursday for dinner then went back to the wards for another shift.

Chapter Ten

Tuesday evening found me sorting through my wardrobe trying to decide what to wear to my dinner engagement with Charles. I had contacted him via my new telephone I had installed and was thrilled to discover he was taking me to the Savoy. I finally decided on the grey chemise and my pearls which I had worn the night of my dinner party. My silver evening bag would complete my ensemble and I would style my hair into a chignon. As I soaked in the bath my thoughts were of Charles. Was he already at Dolphin Square in his pied a terre? What would he be wearing, that grey smoking jacket he had worn at the Hall or a tie and tails? I thought about the Savoy, the two of us at a table for two with a bevy of waiters catering to our needs. My eyes traveled around the bathroom and I compared it to the one I had used at Hagley Hall. That room had been enormous with its claw bath set on black and white tiles, the high ceiling decorated with friezes and the cupboard replete with white fluffy monogrammed towels. Not like the one I was drying myself with now. It was rather thin and was in need of replacement but somehow I had not got around to buying another. My reveries were interrupted by the telephone ringing. With my towel hurriedly wrapped around me, I flew downstairs. To my astonishment and then disappointment it was Charles ringing to apologize saying that he could not keep our dinner arrangement tonight as planned. Something urgent had come up and he had to attend to it. Saying that he would contact me again he then hung up.

ಚ಼ಚ಼ಚ಼

I stood there in my towel, I was so disappointed. I had really looked forward to this night. What could have been so urgent that he had to cancel? Sombrely I went into my bedroom and put away the chemise, the pearls, and the evening bag. I slipped into my nightdress and gown and heated some soup which I had in the kitchen with the wireless on. The BBC was reporting about the situation in Germany. I turned the dial to change the station. I needed something to cheer me up, some lively music not predictions of another war. I found another station, broadcasting from some ballroom in Birmingham. Although the music was not lively at least it was better than the BBC. I sipped my soup and thought at this moment I should be at the Savoy with Charles, dining perhaps on lemon sole followed by some dessert confection all washed down with fine wines. Finishing my soup I made a cup of cocoa then turning off the wireless I went upstairs to bed. Sleep was fitful until the alarm clock sounded on Wednesday morning.

ಐಐಐ

I felt rather down in the dumps at work, my colleagues all noticing I was not my cheerful self. Audrey and Jean felt sorry that my date had been canceled and tried to allay my concern. I took it all on board but went about my duties in a desultory fashion until it was time to depart for home. I was about to take my bag from the locker when I felt a tap on my shoulder. Turning around to my astonishment Charles was standing in front of me with a smile on his face.

"What are you doing here?" I asked.

"I'm here to apologize for standing you up last night and if you do not have anywhere to go would you like to have a bite now?"

I thought about how I looked after a day in the wards. How on earth could I join him for dinner at some exclusive venue? He seemed to sense what I was thinking.

"We don't have to go anywhere too formal as I realize you have been working all day. I thought we might duck into Pall Mall to my club and have a drink or something."

"Oh, alright, Charles, that sounds super but I just need to freshen up." I left him there amid the lockers where he looked rather out of place and ducked into the lavatory. Thank goodness we were not going to the Savoy I thought as I ran a comb through my hair and reapplied

105

some lipstick. I could hardly believe that he was actually here just outside this door.

We walked around to St James Club. The servant at the door enquiring if sir would prefer to sit in one of the drawing rooms first or go straight to the dining room. Charles opted for the latter and we were escorted through the hall, past a staircase and shown to a table in the corner. With large sash windows overlooking Waterloo Gardens the room was airy and spacious albeit with a decided odor of cigars. Dotted around were fusty old men some in chairs with their noses in The Times, glasses of scotch in hand. Others were at tables in earnest conversation probably about the state of the country or world events. I had been something of interest to them when I had walked in dressed in my uniform. Only Charles had some influence with the fellow at the door I might have been forbidden entrance into this hallowed place. I kept thinking the Savoy could not be much grander than this.

ഇരുഇരുഇരു

The waiter came and took our order. He was also appraising me as though I was some foreign object to be dissected under a microscope.

"Don't worry about them," said Charles as he detected my discomfit.

"They are not used to seeing many pretty girls in here."

That relieved my embarrassment and I ignored them instead of concentrating on my white wine which the waiter had promptly brought.

Charles took a sip of his scotch and again apologized for not being able to keep our dinner appointment. He told me he had been summoned urgently to the police station to bail out Bunny who had been arrested for assault. He had been playing whist at Crockford's and had welched on a bet which then resulted in a brawl. The cheek of that man I thought as I listened to the story. Is he never out of trouble? I wondered how many times Charles had come to his aid over the years. I decided to change the subject. I was keen to know more about this man and as this was as good a time as any I asked about his life. He told me he was the only child of lord Davenport of Hagley Hall. He had a nanny called Aggie, went to prep school to finally read history at Oxford. He told me how he hardly saw his mother. She was often confined to bed with migraines and other problems relating to her nerves. Meanwhile, his father was so occupied organizing hunting and shooting parties and eyeing off ladies he did not have much time for his son. I felt sorry for him. Here was I thinking that the only sadness he had was the loss of his wife and child. I had thought he had led a charmed life but it seemed to be far from that. I took another mouthful of wine. I was feeling more relaxed now and the men who had been staring at me before now appeared to have satisfied their curiosity. I started to ask him about Bunny Williams but the waiter approached to take our order for dinner. Charles ordered the fish assuring me it was always rather good here.

"You were asking about Bunny?" Charles said playing with his fork.

"Yes, how long have you known him?"

సోసోసో

He looked across at me and told me that they had been friends since childhood. His father had known his mother and had ensured that the two boys became friends in school. They had been on the same rowing team at Oxford and had remained friends over the years. I thought it was a one-sided friendship. That Bunny seemed to be always taking advantage of Charles' good nature, his kindness and hospitality. I would have loved to tell him about his friend's conduct towards me but now was not the time and maybe there would never be a time. I speared a piece of potato and my eyes traveled to the pictures of racehorses on the wall.

I asked, "Do you ride Charles?" Then, "But I suppose that is a silly question, brought up as you were with hunting and shooting parties on a regular basis."

He met my gaze.

"Yes, but not as much as I used to. I find I don't have the time or inclination."

"Do you?" he asked.

I told him I had a pony when I was a child and competed in gymkhanas, but I had been thrown badly resulting in a broken collarbone and had not been on a horse since.

"Well," he replied, "the best cure for that is to get back into the saddle and start again. When you come to stay I will ask the groom to saddle up a couple and we can go for a canter."

౩౦౩౦౩౦

I visualized myself cantering around with him on the grounds of the estate. Would that ever happen?

"Well," I replied, "if I did muster the courage to resume riding I don't think I will be cantering. Maybe a slow trot would be more my style."

He smiled at that comment then noticing my undisguised yawn Charles summoned the waiter. The account was signed with a flourish and then we were escorted outside where the Rolls Royce awaited. I had thought I would sit in the back which was my usual seat but tonight he seated me in the front with him. We traveled back to my flat our minds enmeshed with our own thoughts. A couple of times I stole a look at him, the strong line of his jaw, his less than perfect nose. David's nose had been aquiline maybe that is what had attracted me in the first place. I had concentrated on superficial beauty and not what lay beneath. Charles caught me looking at him and the smile on his face cracked the carapace which seemingly until now had been enclosing my heart.

"Here we are then, madam, home safe and sound."

He went around to the passenger door and helped me out then walked me to my door.

Should I invite him in I pondered? Would he expect me to? However, fatigue decided for me. I was rather tired and I was sure he would understand. "Now," he said taking my hand, "I have not forgotten about our official dinner at the Savoy."

"Oh, Charles, tonight would have sufficed. It was wonderful. You really don't need to."

He put a finger to my lips to avoid my protestation. "No, he said, "I am a man of my word. What say I make a reservation for tomorrow evening? That is if you are free and you have enough time to select something appropriate to wear."

I accepted his invitation, I could hardly refuse. He took my hand and kissed it then I watched him drive away probably to Dolphin Square. I let myself into the flat and made a cup of cocoa hoping it would have the desired soporific effect however it was a while before I settled as my mind replayed the previous hours I had spent with Charles and my forthcoming dinner with him the following evening.

Chapter Eleven

Since our dinner at the Savoy which had exceeded all my expectations and, to the amusement and delight of my friends, Charles and I had been communicating on a rather regular basis. There had been lots of telephone calls interspersed with the odd tennis party. My prowess with the racquet was not up to Charles' standards as I missed more balls than I hit. However, he thought it was all good fun and I accepted his playful teasing. I was a bit better with croquet finding it more relaxing than tennis, knocking the balls through the hoops after which hot toddies would be served in the drawing room. Maybe it was the thought of that which had me favoring the game. I had said as much to Charles which elicited a laugh. He was laughing a lot more lately. I did not know if it was because of my company or the fact that he was recovering from the deaths of Diana and his child which was now four months ago. In a week it would 1938. We had spent Christmas Day apart as I had committed to be with auntie Eileen at Rachel's in Cambridge. I had not been looking forward to going but apart from auntie, Rachel was my only relative and with the manner in which Hitler was behaving nobody knew if they would see another Christmas. Charles had rung me on Christmas morning to wish me and my family a happy day with advice to ignore Rachel's snide remarks. It took all my efforts to hold back tears as I so wanted to be with him to share the joys of Christmas at Hagley Hall. I had thought about inviting him to come with me but soon abandoned that idea. It would have been too awkward trying to introduce him to Rachel and her lover. Auntie, however, would probably have taken it all in her stride as though it was my custom to be friendly with a lord. He had said it would be a quiet day. Cecily and Tims would be there as well as the colonel and there would be customary gifts exchanged with the servants in front of the Christmas tree. He did not mention if Bunny was to be attending and I did not ask. Before we rang off he told me he had organized a Hogmanay party for New Year's Eve and I was to look forward to that. There would be a fireworks display and something special for me which he hoped would go some way to make up for not seeing each other on Christmas Day. That left me wondering what it could be but it would be enough for me just to be with him.

಄಄಄

Copious libations got me through the lunch at Rachel's. I had managed to incur her wrath as soon as she opened the door. I had thought she had told me to be there at 12.30 but I should have been there one hour later.

"Well, seeing as you're here early you can help prepare the luncheon." She said churlishly hurling an apron at me and pointing to the potatoes which needed peeling.

I set to work and wondered where her lover was as there appeared to be no sign of her. Perhaps my supposition that she lived here was incorrect as I jabbed my finger with the knife. "Is Lucinda coming?" I asked. She finished basting the turkey and pushed it back in the oven.

"Of course, she is coming, she will be here at 1.30, the time I stipulated."

She poured me a glass of sherry which I downed rather quickly trying to quell the feelings my sister always managed to stir in me of inadequacy and mortification. I hoped auntie would arrive soon to be the bulwark of the animosity festering in the kitchen. My prayers were answered when there was a ring at the door and in limped dear auntie Eil encumbered by a string bag of presents. She had been early too as it was only 12.55 but Rachel did not admonish her lack of timing. She instead lavished her with kisses and escorted her into the lounge-room where a fire was burning. Lucinda arrived right at the specified time. Rachel must have her well trained I thought as I downed another sherry while auntie was introduced to her.

"Auntie, this is Lucinda, a good friend of mine." Good friend, I mused, she is more than that. It took lots of restraint not to blurt out that she was her lover. The reaction of auntie would have been priceless as I knew her views on homosexuals, calling them inverts more than once. Gifts were then exchanged in the penumbra of the room, Rachel's economies regarding electricity clearing evident as only one lamp was turned on. It was a dark flat even in the summer located as it was in one of the narrow streets which seldom admitted any sunlight. At least she had purchased some coal to warm the room, I thought otherwise we would be sitting around in our overcoats, scarves, and mittens. Auntie's gifts were distributed first. I had received a lace doily.

"To put under that vase your grandmother gave you, dear."

I had watched for Rachel's reaction as I knew her feelings about that vase. She had been stony-faced. Rachel had received an antimacassar which she had viewed with a slight distaste probably expecting something more modern not this crocheted piece suitable for a grandmother. Lucinda, however, had shown gratitude for her box of Quality Street toffee even opening the tin and handing them around. She was a bit of an improvement on my sister I thought as I popped the toffee into my mouth. It took away the taste of the sherry I had drunk earlier which had tasted rather rank.

"Oh," auntie exclaimed, "handkerchiefs, thank you, dear." I had bought her handkerchiefs with the letter E embroidered on them.

"Well, you can never have too many," I replied. "I am usually losing mine."

I glanced across at Rachel prepared for a snide comment but she was too engrossed in the gift bestowed on her by Lucinda. It was a silver pendant that Rachel promptly fastened around her neck helped by her lover. Rachel gave her a peck on the cheek then rushed over to me and auntie so we could admire the jewelry. She was expecting us to ooh and aah about it but I just put my mouth into a weak smile and gave it a cursory glance. Auntie, however, fingered and examined it saying how lovely it was. Pleased at that reaction she returned to Lucinda and gave a gift to her. I wondered what it would be. She was never noted for her generosity, but she loved and expected people to shower her with presents. Lucinda took her time unwrapping it as though to keep us all in suspense. It was in a small box. Surely it was not a ring she was giving her but then a powder compact was revealed.

"Ooh, I say, smashing," she gushed. She turned it over and discovered her initials engraved on the back. Auntie's embroidered handkerchiefs seemed no match for that and I cringed at the thought. Then Rachel and I swapped gifts. I had bought her an Agatha Christie novel Murder is Easy, which I thought she may enjoy reading on her next overseas trip. There had been mention of a trip to Germany in the near future.

"Oh, actually Peggy, I have read this one but thanks all the same." Was her reply when she had torn off the wrapping. She really knows how to rile me I thought. Imagine saying that to the giver of a present. Even if she had read it she should not have revealed it. Thoroughly fed up I opened her present imagining it would probably be a dried orange or something similar. It was a bottle of Evening In Paris which on closer inspection had already been opened with some of the perfume missing.

"Oh, how generous!" I gushed, racing over and throwing my arms around her in a pretend show of gratitude. "You really went to a lot of trouble." My sarcasm had not been lost and she quickly stood up and announced that lunch would now be served.

ဢဢဢ

We sat around the table pulling crackers. I thought about Charles. Would he be pulling one with Cecily or maybe even Mr. Hudson? Their crackers would be bound to be a higher quality than these as the same old tired jokes were unearthed from their wrappings. We pulled on the paper hats while each of us read these weak words of humor, Lucinda's forced raucous laugh grating in my ears. I placed a piece of turkey and potato onto my fork then noticed a dribble of gravy snaking down my jumper. I quickly wiped it away with the napkin before Rachel had noticed. It would provide her with more ammunition with which to attack me. However, she was too engrossed in promulgating her opinions. I drank some more sauterne, no champagne in sight, and let everything waft over me. In the fog I detected the conversation turning to Hitler and Germany. Both Rachel and her lover seemed to hold the same views. They were sympathetic to the Germans especially Lucinda who expounded that Germany had been very badly treated in the last war. That had not gone over well with auntie who had tried to voice her opinion about all the lives lost in the Great War which was the fault of Germany. However, her opinion did not seem to matter to them, they were so steadfast in their views. I tried to change the subject once or twice about the hospital, the patients even broaching the subject of the King having the option of a Morganatic marriage with Wallis Simpson but the conversation soon reverted to Germany. Then there was a lull as Rachel strode in with the pudding making a big production of pouring over the brandy and setting it alight. It was a good distraction as we all concentrated on finding the pennies lurking in our slices. It was before the tea had been served that auntie took her leave pleading a headache. I knew it was not that. It was the fact she could no longer abide the pro-German discussion and also the fact that Rachel and her friend planned to attend the rally for the fascist Mosley. I had had enough too. I had felt quite unwelcome and was sorry I had come. I could have spent the day with Charles and enjoyed myself. Rachel had not even bothered to ask how I was, so preoccupied was she with that woman. However, that was not unusual as she hardly asked about me most of the time.

ಣಣಣ

Auntie and I both left on the next train for London leaving the Nazi sympathizers to the washing up. Poor auntie seemed astonished that her niece could possess such views.

"I think that friend of hers is a bad influence, Peggy," she said as the train rumbled past Royston. "And," she added, "fancy going to see that nasty man Mosley." But I knew Rachel had always had sympathy for the Germans and did not need much encouragement from anyone else. Maybe that was their shared interest, what had drawn them to each other in the first place. They had probably met at one of those fascist meetings. As the train stopped at Walton-at-Stone, I thought I would tell auntie about Charles. It would take her mind off Rachel's behavior.

"Oh, that's lovely for you dear," she said, "I hope he treats you better than that other fellow you took up with." She was talking about David. I was not aware that she had known but as she and mother had always been close, mother had obviously confided in her.

"Oh, auntie, he is so unlike him. He is kind and considerate, a real gentleman," I enthused. "I am certain you would like him."

"Well, that is good to hear, Peggy. I should look forward to meeting him one day that is if you have not moved on to someone else. You young ones can be so fickle."

I thought that would never happen. I could never entertain the idea of being with anyone else and then worriedly I thought what if he wants to move on to someone else?

Chapter Twelve

My fears were allayed at the New Year's Eve party. As soon as Bill opened the car door Charles came rushing out to greet me. All my concerns faded away as he swept me into his arms and I felt his lips on mine. Arm in arm we entered the house as Hudson divested me of my coat and my suitcase. All the lights and lamps were turned on highlighting the tinsel and holly which was wound around the giant staircase and in pride of place stood the huge Christmas tree soaring to the ceiling. With its red and silver baubles and a glittering star on top it was just what I had visualized.

"Oh, Charles," I gasped, "it is all so superb."

"It is rather, isn't it?" he replied as we both stood admiring it. "The staff always come up trumps every year with the decos."

From the drawing room, there was the hum of people and I wondered who would be here at this party. I hoped that Bunny would be a no show. Charles had not mentioned if he would be coming.

Charles turned to me and said, "Go up and change while I rustle up something to drink then meet me in the library."

I was puzzled why we were not going to join the others but I did as he suggested and made my way to the bedroom. I was getting used to this room as I had slept there more than once, and Hudson was now used to me popping up from London for the odd weekend. However, I was unsure of the housekeeper, she still seemed to have an aversion towards me. I took my dress from the case and put it on. It was a long cocktail dress fitted at the top with shoestring straps and fell from the waist in folds of glittering gold and red. It was another of my bargain buys on the high street. I thought it looked rather festive especially for a New Year party and hoped the neckline was not displaying too much decolletage. I arranged my hair into a chignon as I knew Charles approved of that style commenting more than once it had highlighted my cheekbones. I reapplied more lipstick and dabbed some perfume behind my ears and on my wrists. I arrived in the library to find a fire was burning in the grate and the mantelpiece was festooned with sprigs of holly and Christmas cards. I really love this room I thought as I walked towards the massive floor to ceiling bookcases. My finger stroked the golden spine of one which I noticed was a Dickens' classic. I envisioned whiling away the hours with a novel as Hudson or the footman brought me tea and scones. During the times I had stayed at the Hall that had been what I had not received. It had always been drinks and cigarettes.

ಬಿಬಿಬಿ

Charles came in carrying an ice bucket containing what looked like a bottle of champagne and two glasses. He closed and locked the door then placed the bucket on the table near the fireplace. He came towards me.

"I thought champagne might be appropriate," he said

"Well," I commented with a smile, "It is New Year's Eve after all."

He did not reply but took the glasses and poured a little champagne into each. He placed the bottle back in the bucket. Then he gathered me into his arms and his mouth sought mine.

He smelt of sandalwood with a touch of spice.

"Happy new year," I said rather breathless as we drew apart.

"No, darling, this is not to do with the New Year but I hope there will be lots of happy years ahead of us. The thing is..."

"Yes, Charles?"

"Peggy, darling Peggy, I love you, could you, would you marry me?"

I could not believe what I had just heard, Charles asking me to marry him. There was not a word to brand the moment. It was a balm to my soul and my heart.

"Oh, yes, yes, darling I will, of course, I will marry you." I felt tears of joy running down my cheeks. It was probably creating rivulets in the face powder I had carefully applied but I did not care, I was so happy. He wanted me and no one else.

He breathed a sigh of relief. He had been unsure of my answer.

"Didn't you think I would say yes?" I asked him as we sat on the chaise sipping our now most needed champagne, a vintage Louis Roederer.

"I was not certain. I did not know if you would want to be with a crusty old man of 31 with a few gray hairs coming to the fore."

"Crusty old man? I chortled. "What rubbish, you are far from that and I must say I have rather a penchant for older men."

"And, what about me? I am not a blushing virgin." I reminded him. As I said that I had wished I was. I would have loved to be coming to him on our wedding night, pure and chaste but I had been married and that could not be changed, however, if we could restrain ourselves until the wedding maybe that would be a compromise. I proposed the idea to him but as his kisses became more fervent he murmured huskily he would not be making promises he knew he would break.

We stayed in the library for awhile not wanting anything to break the magic of our special time the only sound was the coal shifting in the grate.

"I suppose we had better join the party, darling," he said rising from the chaise and helping me up.

"Everyone will wonder what has happened to my host. But, before we do here is your somewhat belated Christmas present." He withdrew from the pocket of his jacket a black velvet box and opened it to reveal a diamond bracelet.

"Oh, darling it is magnificent," I cried.

"It should have been a diamond ring," he said putting it around my wrist and fastening the clasp." but I was unsure of your size, however, we will take a trip into Hancocks and you can select something to your liking."

I held it up, its colors sparkled in the lamplight. I thought of what I had bought him. They were a set of cuff links marked down to half price in Selfridges. They were certainly not of the standard of this bracelet.

"I have your present upstairs in my bag but I'm afraid it will not be anything as expensive as this."

He waved away my concerns. I was the only present he was interested in.

We left the sanctity of the library and walked out towards the drawing room.

"Are we going to announce our engagement tonight?" I whispered.

"I thought it might be an opportune time after 12.00 on New Year's Day when all the gaiety has subsided. What do you think?"

I replied that I wanted the whole world to know and share the happiness I was feeling.

The drawing room was devoid of guests as they had now moved on to the dining room. As we entered I cast my eye around for Bunny but fortunately he was absent however there were familiar faces in the assemblage at whom I nodded and waved: Cecily, Tims, the tennis players, Mary and George and the colonel to whom Charles introduced me. With his clipped mustache and ramrod straight back he certainly looked an ex-army type. Tims seemed a very nice sort of fellow. I had spoken to him briefly at the funeral. He had said he was a dentist and was between relationships. Charles had told me his girlfriend had been two-timing him so he had sworn off women for a while.

I sat next to Charles who was apologizing to everyone for his tardiness saying he had something to sort out in the library. That brought rather a smile to my face and under cover of the table I gave his leg a squeeze.

With its crystal glasses glinting in the light of the candelabra the table looked its magnificent self. Adding to the festiveness were sprigs of holly while red and green streamers interspersed with gold balloons reigned overhead. I hoped there would be other nights like this but with the talk of war circulating I was not so sure. The footman and Hudson came through with the first course which was mousse a la Florentine, followed by roast turkey, potatoes and all the trimmings. The turkey reminded me of Christmas lunch, of the potatoes I had peeled on the order of my sister. I should have refused. Who did she think she was ordering me about like I was some wayward child or her servant? But I had held my tongue, kept the peace, did not make waves just as I usually do.

"A penny for your thoughts, sweetness," said Charles bringing me out of my reveries as dessert was being handed around.

"Oh, plum pudding," I exclaimed as my eyes alighted on the dish. "This has been just like Christmas Day."

"That is because I instructed Mrs. O'Hara," he replied with a grin "I wanted to make up for the fact you were not here on the day."

How considerate he was to think of that, my darling kind Charles. He would make a great father. I hoped he would want to have a family after losing his, but maybe if there is a war he may not want to bring a child into such a world. After losing my baby I desperately wanted another and as soon as possible. I had mentioned to him once that I had miscarried but he was unaware of the circumstances. I would tell him one day when the time was right and I felt comfortable doing so. I had a chance to ask him about Bunny's whereabouts as it was unusual that he was not here. Charles had replied that he had gone to India to source more cotton and then was going on to America to look into a new machine that was coming on to the market. I felt rather relieved that I would not have to be accosted by him any time soon.

It was 11.50 when the dinner was completed and everyone adjourned to the terrace to watch the fireworks display. I took my shawl to guard against the cold night air, and, as midnight exploded in a bang and rockets lit up the sky and after Auld Lang Syne had been sung Charles announced to the throng our wonderful news.

Chapter Thirteen

It was the 3rd of January 1938 and I was back at St Margaret's. After all the excitement and festivities, I had needed an extra day to recover. We had danced until the dawn of New Year's Day the others having gone home or to bed. The song, The Very Thought of You now firmly imprinted on my mind as Charles had held me close, humming the words and whispering love in my ear. He had tried to hire his sax player and the band but they had a previous commitment in London so the gramophone had been put into service.

Bleary-eyed at breakfast, we had confronted Hudson who again had offered us his warmest congratulations calling me your ladyship and bobbing his head. I shall have to get used to being called that I thought as I helped myself to scrambled eggs and bacon. I could not believe how hungry I was. Maybe it was because of the happiness engulfing me or the fact that I had overindulged in the champagne which flowed endlessly last night. I looked over at Charles who had also heaped his plate with the same fare although he had added mushrooms and kippers and was tucking in with gusto.

"Don't forget about the picnic by the river later your lordship," said Hudson casting his eye over our huge breakfast cognisant that we were not leaving much room for our lunch.

"Yes, thank you, Hudson we won't forget." As he walked out of the room to collect the black tea we had ordered Charles put down his knife and fork and meeting my gaze told me how much he loved me even though I looked a little worse for wear. I riposted back that he could speak for himself and we were both laughing when Hudson returned with the tea. I did enjoy our good-natured banter, the playful teasing and I hoped it would always be like this then I thought of the war, surely it would not happen. The Great War was supposed to be a war that ended all wars. I was placing that concern into the outer reaches of my mind as Charles suggested a stroll around the grounds to walk off our breakfast and clear our heads. There had been no sign of the other guests. They were obviously in no state to face the public and I supposed we would see them later at the picnic. Cecily had not been overly enthusiastic about our news. I presumed she was still in grief about Diana. I conveyed my feelings to Charles as we sat in the gazebo, the same one in which I had sat when Charles was ill in bed. How much time had passed since then and how many things had happened?

"Oh, darling, she will come around. She likes you, you know." He had said looking into my eyes and squeezing my hand.

I looked down and then met his gaze

"I do hope so, and I like her. Oh, Charles, do you think it is all too soon for us?" Do you think we should have waited a bit longer?"

He picked up a leaf that had blown in. It was turning brown and dried around the edges. He looked at it as if it would give him an answer. Then he scrunched it in his hand.

"I don't think she ever loved me you know."

"Who?"

"Diana."

"Diana, what do you mean?"

Then it all came forth, the posy and the card left on the grave, the woman who had placed it there, her lover, Arabella, daughter of the earl of Walsham. He told me the marriage had turned out to be a sham as Diana had been seeing this woman during the marriage. He had thought that a baby might have brought her around, might have put a stop to her philandering but it had all been a disaster. She had not wanted a child, she had intended to leave Charles and live with her lover in a stone cottage in the woods of Kent, the cottage which Charles presumed to have been their love nest, where Diana had gone when she was supposed to be visiting her ailing mother. A week before the fatal accident there had been a showdown. Charles had put forth a compromise. She could still see Arabella and remain married to him and he would engage a nanny to look after the child. However, this was not to Diana's liking. She wanted a complete separation, a divorce, even taking the blame as the guilty party if that was what it would take. He said to this day, Cecily nor anybody else was aware there had been anything amiss as in public the two of them had performed as the happy couple expecting a baby.

I had been dumbstruck. I did not know what to say except to hold his hand and put my arm around him. Here was I thinking about his charmed life, his happy marriage to Diana when all the while she had taken a lover and a woman at that. There seemed to be a lot of these kinds of relationships occurring, my sister and her lover, Diana and hers.

"I'm so sorry, darling," I whispered finally feeling the urge to speak

Another leaf blew in this one was fresh and green. I hoped it was a portent of the future, a fresh start for us.

"The two of us seem to have things in common," I said looking into his eyes which to my dismay still bore traces of sadness.

"What's that?"

"My sister has a lover too."

"Oh?"

"Yes, she was at the Christmas lunch, she works as a secretary for someone in the Admiralty and is a Nazi sympathizer just like Rachel."

He brightened a little. It took his mind off what he just related to me.

I continued to regale him about the lunch, the appalling way Rachel had treated me especially the gift of the used perfume. That had brought forth a chortle for which I was grateful. I hated to see my darling enmeshed in sadness. I wanted to hear him laughing and gay just as he was last night.

Consulting his watch, he thought we should be heading back. Hudson would be displeased if we were to arrive late for the picnic and that would never do. I thought of the displeasure also of Mrs. Keen and her attitude towards me. She had admonished me once for wearing my tiny diamond earrings, "A lady should never wear diamonds in the country madam," she had said. Then I thought what her reaction would be if she sighted the diamond bracelet which was on my wrist. It made me feel a little smug. She could hardly tell me off about that if the master of the house had given it to me. I walked with Charles hand in hand back across the grounds, towards the picnic location, the bracing air going some way dispelling what Charles had related to me.

By the banks of the river lazing on rugs and deckchairs, we found our guests already partaking of the food and wine which had been transported by the staff from the house.

We found a spot for ourselves on the outer rim of a rug as everyone greeted and again congratulated us apart from the colonel who was clearly asleep with his mouth open, a half-empty bottle of hock lying beside him. The conversation was desultory, everyone not yet fully recovered from the night before. Charles poured me a wine which was nicely chilled and we helped ourselves to chicken legs. I looked over at Mary and George who were presently canoodling on the rug and it took a lot of effort to stop myself from pushing Charles down and canoodling with him but it would have been inappropriate. Mary and George seemed content. They reminded me of Audrey and Edward however from what Charles had told me who knew what went on in a marriage? Who knew what went on behind closed doors? Who knew what had gone in my marriage to David? As I was contemplating that the colonel had stirred from his slumber. He ambled over to us.

"Well, lovely day for the picnic," he said plonking himself beside Charles.

"Did you enjoy the fireworks last night little lady?"

"They were outstanding, colonel and I was so pleased the night was fine."

"One can always rely on a good party at the Hall especially on New Year's Eve."

"Do you usually attend every year?" I asked him as I sipped my wine my other hand being held by Charles.

"Yes, if I can make it. However last year I was laid up with a dose of gout. Do you remember Charles?"

"Yes, colonel I do, and I think it was the middle of January when you were up and about."

You should try and restrict the alcohol," Charles advised.

"I think it's a bit late for that old chum," replied the colonel as he took a glass pouring into it a good measure of sauterne. "Can't abide all that balderdash," he added.

I liked the colonel. He was a straight shooter and stuck to his convictions. He would enjoy whatever life he had left whatever the consequences. I noticed that Tims had taken the dinghy which had been tied up at the bank and was rowing along the river and wondered if he had been on the same rowing team as Charles. I felt rather sorry for Tims as I waved to him, he probably felt the odd one out as apart from the colonel he was not part of a couple. It would be lovely if he could find someone else, some nice girl with whom to share his life.

The afternoon slumbered on and the sun had set by the time we all made our way back to the house. We spent the rest of the night playing charades and generally larking about until it was time for everyone to fall into bed and it took a lot of restraint on both of us to sleep in our own rooms. However, as I was so exhausted after no sleep the previous night I do not think even Charles could have induced me into doing anything of a sexual nature. The next day Bill had been seconded to drive me home as Charles had a meeting with a roofer who was quoting to fix the dry rot. Prior to that in the confines of the library, Charles and I discussed the date and venue of our wedding. The library was turning out to be my favorite room as apart from its atmosphere and the books it contained there was also the memory of Charles' proposal.

"I think it should be in July," he had said consulting the calendar, "and we can honeymoon in Europe for a couple of months."

"What do you think?"

"It sounds wonderful darling, perfect. I love summer weddings." I was envisioning the gown I would wear. When I married David I just threw on a suit and a cloche hat, the only concession to a bit of frippery was a feather on the side of it. He said we would honeymoon in Europe. I could hardly believe it, Charles and I taking in the sights as husband and wife.

"You look a million miles away," he said breaking into my thoughts "You would not be thinking of your wedding gown by any chance."

"How did you know?'

"Isn't that what all girls think of when they marry?"

"Yes," I laughed "You win. I was thinking of that and also going to Europe."

Then he asked me where I would want the wedding, here at the Hall or somewhere else.

I had thought about having it here, we had the staff for the catering but I had heard this is where he had married Diana. It might stir up memories and I did not want anything to ruin our special day.

"Darling," I said touching his hand which still held the pencil.

"As lovely as the Hall is, I really would like to marry somewhere else, however, it is rather a long way from here."

"Oh, and where would that be?"

"France."

"France?"

"Yes, darling. There is a place in the Dordogne, a beautiful place called Rocamadour."

"Oh, yes I know the area," he replied, "I have actually acquired a few antiques around those parts."

Pleased that he knew of the location and warming to my theme I continued, "There is a beautiful chapel right at the top of the cliff with steps leading up and embedded in the steps are tiny shells placed there by pilgrims centuries ago."

"How do you know so much about this place?" he asked now quite interested.

"It was where my grandmother married."

"Oh, was she French?"

"No, she wasn't. She married a French diplomat and they lived in Sarlat, a village not far from Rocamadour."

"Oh, did she now? Well, seeing as you seem to have your heart set on going there who am I to deny you?"

I sprang from the chair and threw my arms around him nearly knocking over the lamp in the process.

"Oh, do you really mean it? I exclaimed covering him with kisses. "Oh, Charles thank you."

I was ecstatic. I would be married in that holy chapel, the one I had heard so much about. Then he had another idea. He knew of a chateau not far from Rocamadour and he would make inquiries about holding our reception there. We both wanted our wedding to be intimate only inviting a few friends and relatives. He had said his wedding to Diana had been over the top, a society wedding with hundreds of guests attending with a mention in the social column of The Times. I cast my mind back to see if I remembered reading anything about it but we had not bought The Times, it was always The Daily Telegraph David had insisted on.

Then Hudson appeared to advise Charles that the dry rot man was downstairs, so our discussion was postponed for another day. At least there had been plans made and it was those thoughts that accompanied me on the drive home with Bill.

Now here I was in the sluice room far away from Hagley Hall and France. I knew Jean and Audrey would be trying to track me down bombarding me with questions they not knowing that I was engaged to be married to Charles. Every time I thought of it I felt a frisson of happiness and I was in disbelief that it was all real and not something I had dreamt.

"Ah, here you are, the prodigal returns," announced Audrey pouncing on me. I put the pan down washed my hands and gave her a hug.

"Yes, I suppose you could call me that, as that is how I feel, rather self-indulgent."

"Well, what's news?" How was the party at the mansion?"

I looked around the door to see if matron was in the vicinity.

"If you're looking for matron she is ill," said Audrey

"Oh?"

"Yes, her kidney stones were playing up again. Her replacement isn't much better but at the moment she is trying to get her head around some paperwork, so the coast is clear for gossip."

I would have to tell matron I would be leaving and tender my resignation I thought as we headed off to the tea room. We found Jean feet up, cigarette in hand and a cup of tea beside her.

As soon as she saw me she leaped off the chair.

"Oh, Peg. It's so good to see you again," she said enfolding me in a hug.

"Now sit down and tell us all the gossip, sordid or otherwise."

In the fog of cigarettes and the odor of stewed tea, I related my news.

"Oh, Peg, didn't I say about cupid slinging his bow?" Jean exclaimed, "I am so happy for you."

"You deserve it Peg," enthused Audrey, "you deserve every happiness, I am dying to meet him."

They bombarded me with their questions both talking at the same time they were so excited. When was the wedding? Where would it be? They could hardly believe it when I told them we would be holding it in July in France at Rocamadour, with the reception in a chateau.

"Blimey," cried Jean on to her third cigarette, her tea cold in the cup, "it's just like Hollywood!"

Making the most of matron's absence, we stayed a while longer and over fresh tea and biscuits, I heard what my friends had been up to over the Christmas season. Audrey and Edward had decided to go back to the Hotel in Scotland and Jean had gone to stay with her parents which she said she had regretted. Her Christmas lunch had been worse than mine as her father had got into a political argument with his brother punching him in the mouth and knocking out two teeth. "And," she said, "Grannie never stopped asking me when I was getting married, I tell you it will be the last time I go there at Christmas. I would have been better off at my place listening to the wireless and having beans on toast." There was laughter all around and then I told them of my experience. "Fancy giving you a used bottle of perfume, Peg, that really takes the cake!" commented Audrey. They were aware of my sister's behavior towards me, Jean thanking her stars that she had a brother who always looked after her. He was the one who had stepped in to try and break up the fight, shielding her from their father's raised fist.

Audrey commented philosophically that you can pick your friends but not your family to which I replied: "Amen to that."

We finished our tea and gossip and decided we had better make tracks. I headed off to the antenatal while Audrey and Jean went to women's surgical.

As I entered the ward I noticed Mrs. Watts had returned. Surely she was not pregnant again!

"Oi, nursie, over here," she yelled

I walked to her bed

"What are you doing here again?"

She pulled herself up and related her tale of woe

"I was havin' the seventh but I lost it. To tell you the truth, between you and me and it was just as well as I couldn't have looked after another one. Me Bert don't make much money on those docks, strugglin' to feed us all so he is. The house is near burstin' at the seams. The kids are sleepin' head to tail. Oh, it's real hard so it is." She was sniveling and wiping her nose on the sheet.

I put my arm around her shoulder

"There, now, don't upset yourself," I said "How about I make you a nice cuppa and maybe a biscuit to go with it?"

She brightened at that suggestion so I hurried off to the kitchen returning with the tea and a ginger nut.

"Ooh, that's good, that is," she said slurping the tea and dunking the biscuit.

"Yes, I find a cup of tea seems to make everything better."

I thought I would give her some good news, something to take her mind off her troubles so I pulled up a chair.

"Do you want to hear something nice?" I asked.

She put the cup and saucer on the table.

"Oh, yes dearie, I could do with hearing somethin' good and no mistake."

I leaned towards her.

"Well, I have just become engaged to a lord and I will be leaving the hospital to live in a grand house in Bedfordshire."

Her eyes lit up.

"You never are marryin' one of 'em lords," she spluttered.

"Well, I never. Wait til' I tell me, neighbors. That'll give 'em somethin' to talk about besides drunk 'usbands and screamin' kids. You will make a lovely bride, dearie. Your lord is a lucky man."

She patted my hand then said, "I hopes you have a happy life."

"Thank you so much, Mrs. Watts. Now if you have finished with the tea, see if you can have a little nap."

Settling her under the sheet I took the cup and saucer the latter containing the tea which she had spilled in her merriment. I was walking towards the door when I heard her shout to all and sundry,

"Oi, everyone, our nursie is marryin' a lord!"

Poor Mrs. Watts, I thought en route to the kitchen. At least I brought her some happiness albeit transitory. It must be so hard for women like her struggling to care for numerous children with scarce resources. As I washed the crockery I hoped that this pregnancy would be her last.

Chapter Fourteen

The weeks passed in the lead up to our wedding and tonight we were hosting a cocktail party at the Hall for our closest friends. Audrey, Edward, and Jean had motored up but aunt Eileen's sciatica had precluded her from coming. She had been rather chuffed when I had rung her with the news and said if she had to be in a wheelchair she would not miss my wedding. Also, Cecily had been a no show pleading a migraine and I wondered if that was true. I so wanted us to be friends as we had been before. It was not our fault that her daughter had died, as tragic as it was. Surely she could not deny Charles a chance at happiness especially with another war looming on the horizon. She had not even been aware of Diana's unfaithfulness, her intention of leaving Charles for a woman the fact about which would have been horrified. Audrey and Jean had been ecstatic about the ring which Charles has purchased at Hancock's. It was a simple design, an oval-shaped solitaire diamond on a gold band. "Understated elegance," were Audrey's words as she examined it in the confines of Mirabelle where she Jean and I had a pre-wedding dinner. They were quite lost for words when I recounted my shopping expedition with Charles. The visit to an exclusive French lingerie shop for the purchasing of silk and lace confections for my trousseau. The selection at Selfridges of my cream bridal gown which was long and satin with a boat neckline set off by a veil. Jean had been pleased about that mirthfully saying Charles could lift it to look into my eyes. They were thrilled at the prospect of being bridesmaids albeit Audrey who was classified as matron of honor and there was an appointment made at Selfridges for the fitting of their gowns. I had given Rachel the option but knew it would have been anathema to her which it was as she had pointed out to me on the phone, "Oh, I don't think so, all that sugary sentimentality, brides done up like meringues, anyway," she had added, "I shall be in Germany by then so am afraid I will miss the betrothal altogether." Just like her, I had fumed, not even bothering to attend her only sister's wedding. I was probably better off without her, she would have ruined the day finding something about which to criticize. No, I would be more relaxed with my friends. I had purposefully allocated a fitting time to coincide with their lunch breaks as I did not us to incur the wrath of matron. I had told her I was to be married and had tendered my resignation and I felt rather moved when she gave me a hug and wished me much happiness for the future. She was not such a bad old stick, I thought, her bark was worse than her bite.

After shopping and the packages had been placed in the car, we had lunch at Charles' club. This time the club servant treated me with more respect and the fusty old diners barely raised an eyebrow as we were escorted to our table, the same one at which I had shyly sat that night in my nurse's uniform. During lunch, my eyes kept straying to the ring as it glistened in the sunlight stealing through the window. It was my first engagement ring as there had been no engagement with David, only that hasty registry office betrothal.

Charles had been trying hard to keep his promise of celibacy. Dropping me at my place and returning to his den, keeping temptation at bay. I wondered if I was being silly about it. After all, I had been married and so had he and we were engaged but I still wanted our wedding night to be special and I knew it would be worth waiting for.

ℤℤℤ

The strains of Billy Holiday wafted across the room as Henry, the footman and Hudson glided around with trays of martinis and canapes. I whispered to Charles that Tims and Jean seemed to be getting along as I saw her a couple of times throw her head back in laughter at a joke he had told her. Maybe cupid would sling his bow her way this time.

She, Audrey and Edward had been in awe of the house when we had shown them around all in disbelief at the immensity of it. As Charles was relating the history, how in 1600 it had been built with modifications added through the centuries, I noticed Audrey hanging on his every word and I knew she had approved of him, my fiancé. I had left Charles sharing a whiskey with Edward while I took my friends to walk through the maze however our navigations proved unsuccessful and it was Mr. Mullins who heard our cries for help dropping his spade and coming to our rescue.

"You lassies want to be careful of this old maze," he had said leading us out "I heard tell someone got lost in there one day and it was three days until he was found."

With furrowed brows, we had looked at each other not knowing if that was a myth or a truth but, until it was confirmed, I determined to keep my distance.

In the drawing room, the rugs had now been rolled back and it was to the strains of Duke Ellington that we kicked up our heels and had some fun. As I danced the rumba with Charles I tried to put the thoughts of war from my mind. It was always in the papers, Hitler, the mistreatment of the jews, their segregation, the Sudetenland crisis. I cast my mind to happier things, to our forthcoming wedding in Rocamadour in the holy chapel up in the clouds, our reception in the chateau and then Europe. Charles had said after France we would go to Rome and to Venice and I felt my heart leap visualizing us in each other's arms in a gondola floating down one of the canals in the moonlight. David and I did not have a honeymoon. We had gone from the registry office to Brighton, to a dank lodging house which someone had recommended, and it was our home until we parted. One day I would tell Charles about that other life when I had the courage when the time was right. How different this marriage would be I thought as we glided around the room, his cheek brushing mine, his strong arms holding me close. I wanted at that moment to feel his lips on mine tasting his sweetness. Could I last the distance until our wedding?

When the martinis were drunk, the canapés were eaten and the gramophone silenced, everyone retired for the night. It took all my self-control not to burst into Charles' room and leap into his bed. However, I knew that the next time I would see him would be in the chapel in France when he would be my husband and it was the thought of that which transported me into a dreamless sleep.

Chapter Fifteen

It was July 3rd, 1938 in Rocamadour. I slipped the white satin bridal gown over my head and knew it would not be long until I was standing beside my darling reciting our vows in the holy chapel on the cliff. With ambivalent emotions, I had given up the lease on my flat. I would certainly miss it as it had been my home its walls privy to my thoughts and feelings both dark and light, however, my future was with Charles as mistress of Hagley Hall. Matron had organized a farewell in the tea room and had passed the hat around for a collection from the staff. I had been presented with a vanity bag "To take on your honeymoon dear," she had said. I felt very touched by everyone's generosity and good wishes which were all written on a farewell and good luck card. Charles and Tims had flown to France a few days before the wedding. First to Paris to confirm the delivery of the flowers from Les Jardins, an exclusive florist on Rue des Rosiers, thence they were driven to Rocamadour to the hotel in which we were all staying. Tims had been excited at the prospect of being the best man as Bunny apparently was still away on business. That fact I had been happy about as I was sure he would have behaved inappropriately and probably ruined the wedding. Cecily, auntie Eil together with Audrey, Edward and Jean all traveled with me on the boat train and after the ferry journey, we were collected by limousines for our journey to Rocamadour. George and Mary had also gone on ahead as Mary had a cousin living outside Paris and wanted to visit her. I felt disappointed that the colonel's gout prevented him from attending. He was a good old stick and I liked him very much. I had not been keen on flying and neither had auntie as we knew the turbulence would result in one or other of us having to use the sick bowls. More than one prayer had been offered by me to keep Charles and Tims safe as their plane flew up and over the channel on their way to France. However, we all enjoyed our land journey especially the drive from Paris to the Dordogne valley. En route, the chauffeur had informed us that the surrounding cliffs contained caves that contained rock art drawn by prehistoric man and the drawings even now were very bright and legible.

I thought maybe Charles and I could explore one of these caves before visiting Sarlat, the village where Grandma lived all those years ago. Charles had said we would go there after our honeymoon and try to locate the house in which she had lived. From the back seat, I could hear Cecily and auntie conversing. I thought Cecily may have been a bit too high brow for aunt but there they were chatting away about art and the latest movies interspersed with their physical complaints and their tips for remedies of the same. Cecily was quite into various charitable causes and was asking auntie if she would be interested in supporting any. Audrey, Edward, and Jean were enjoying the whole experience trying out their minimal knowledge of the French language on the chauffeur everyone dissolving into laughter at the mispronunciation of the words. I had schoolgirl French, rather basic, just enough to perhaps order un cafe or des croissants. I would have to let Charles be the converser as having traveled here on business on many occasions he was more fluent in the language. I thought of him whispering in French, Je t'adore. It sounded so romantic. Perhaps I would ask him if he would oblige.

"You look stunning," exclaimed Jean as she put the finishing touches to my veil. "You will really knock Charles' eyes out when he sees you."

"And with that tiara," added Audrey, You could easily pass for a princess," Charles had given me the diamond tiara which had been handed down his family through the generations. I thought if I am lucky enough to have a daughter she would be able to also wear it on her wedding day.

It was time to go, to leave the hotel, go out into the sunshine and walk the way of the pilgrims up the steps to the chapel where my beloved was waiting.

Audrey and Jean attended to the train and with the rest of the veil over my face and the bouquet of baby's breath, forget-me-nots, and sweet peas, I and my bridesmaids commenced the bridal procession. Through the street full of well-wishers we walked then slowly up the ancient steps embedded with the shells of the pilgrims. I thought of Grandma, of her wedding here, if she had been as happy as I was or as excited. From above I heard the call of an osprey. Was it a sign of a happy future, was it wishing me well? Then its sound was surpassed as the notes of Ave Maria rent the air and I was entering the door of the chapel. Audrey accompanied me down the tiny aisle and then there I was beside my darling whose face could not disguise the joy he was feeling. "You look beautiful," I heard him whisper his hand quickly dashing away a tear that had escaped onto his cheek. I loved him so much. I loved the way he was not afraid to show his emotions. He grasped my hand tightly as if to prevent me from walking away.

The priest commenced the service and we knelt down at the altar glowing with candlelight. Charles gently lifted the veil from my face and with trembling voice, I took him to be my husband, to love, cherish and obey, in sickness and in health, until death do us part.

He placed the ring on my finger then looking with adoration into my eyes he also said his vows. It was done, we were married. I felt like a queen as we walked together from that ancient chapel as confetti rained down on us and we continued with our friends towards the chateau, the venue of our reception.

Chandeliers twinkled above as we seated ourselves in the oak-paneled dining room and I thought it was not dissimilar to the room in Hagley Hall. The menu, however, was, as pate de foie gras, and confit of duck was decidedly french. A three-piece orchestra was playing french songs, songs of love. I looked at Charles beside me and he returned my gaze, his smiling eyes confirming how much I loved him, this dear man who had entered my life. I wondered what he was thinking. Would it be what I was thinking about the consummation later of our marriage upstairs in the bridal suite? I took my glass and swallowed more champagne. It was working its magic, calming, relaxing me. Please god, let him not be disappointed in me. Please let me enjoy my darling's love tonight and block out all bad memories.

Charles put down his knife and fork.

"Darling," he said taking my hand "I believe this is our dance. Let's give them something to talk about."

I walked with him to the center of the floor and to the strains of Begin the Beguine Charles took me in his arms and held me so close I could hear the beating of his heart. The smell of his cologne was intoxicating and I felt oblivious to everyone and everything in the room. It was just us in our own world and I wanted to stay like this forever. The music ended. It was time for us to cut our cake. Three tiers high with tiny red rosebuds had been ordered by Charles from Patisserie Stohrer in the 1st arrondissement in Paris. Sharing the knife we sliced into it and the waiters bustled over cutting up slices to be handed around to our guests.

Everyone seemed to be enjoying themselves especially Jean and Tims who had taken to the dance floor and to my surprise even auntie was there with Edward who had kindly asked her for a tentative twirl. I was so pleased that she had been able to attend. She was my only relative who was at my wedding. I wished Rachel and I had been on good terms and she could have come. I wondered about her in Germany, in Berlin with that lover of hers. She said that Lucinda had to travel there to undertake research for her book but I did not know what the book was about as she had not bothered to tell me and I had not asked. I thought of Charles not having any relatives here only Cecily and she could not be counted being the mother in law. We certainly seemed to have things in common in that respect.

"Bye, have a lovely time," cried Audrey. It was time for us to leave. The reception was over.

"Don't do anything I wouldn't do," quipped Jean. She whispered that she and Tims had decided to spend a couple of days in Paris together taking in the sights before returning to London.

"Take care now Peggy dear," said Aunt "And mind out for those Italians. They don't behave as properly as us English."

Edward pecked me on the cheek and wished me well then shook hands with Charles.

After receiving hugs from Mary, George, and Cecily, the latter's attitude towards me had thankfully reverted to what it was prior to our engagement, I turned around and threw my bouquet. It was caught by Jean whose squeals of joy signified how lucky she felt.

We left our guests for the remainder of the night. They would return to the hotel and head back tomorrow to Paris then home to London. Alone in our tower room, Charles took my hand and walked me over to the mullion window which overlooked the moat encircling the chateau.

"Look, darling, there is a dinghy," he said, "Maybe tomorrow I can see if my rowing skills are still up to speed and I can take us out on the moat."

"Alright," I said, "As long as I don't tip us over and we land in the drink."

"Well then, I would jump in and come to your rescue. I seem to be rather good at rescuing you from calamity don't I?"

I playfully dug him in the ribs.

"Yes, I suppose you do have that reputation. You are my knight in shining armor."

"I think this knight's armor should come off," he said slowly shrugging out of his jacket, pulling off his shirt and tie.

I was glad he was delaying, not ripping off my clothes, not pushing me onto the bed as David had done. He placed his clothes on the nearby chair then carefully removed my tiara and the veil and placed them carefully on top.

He took my face in his hands and looked tenderly into my eyes then I felt his mouth on mine tasting his sweetness, drowning in his love. I felt a stirring in the pit of my stomach and I was ready for him to undo the buttons of my gown and slip it over my head. He planted fairy kisses on my neck then slowly pulled down the straps of my camisole. He undid my bra and let it drop to the floor and then I was standing before him my breasts exposed. His head dropped and he sucked my nipples and with his hand kneaded me through the silk of my panties. Oh, the feeling was sublime. I wanted him so badly. He removed his trousers and I could see his erection. He led me to the bed and laid me gently down. He removed his underwear then removed mine. We were now completely naked and I knew our marriage would soon be consummated in this French chateau in the valley of the Dordogne. I was ready for him, ready for his seed. His sweet lips were on mine, his tongue gently explored my mouth, his hand hardened my nipples.

"Oh, now darling, please come to me now," I cried. He entered me and we were one and pleasure was my only thought as I held him tightly until his passion was spent. He kissed me again and rolled off me onto his side of the bed. He held my hand, my eyes were closed. We lay there in silence both reliving the moment of our love, the only sound, the soughing of the trees outside the window. Then he turned me onto my stomach and he was behind me. It was then the nightmare surfaced, the nightmare that was David, the monster. I screamed and rolled over.

"No, no, please not like that,"

"What is it darling?" Charles asked, "What's wrong?" He maneuvered himself around to face me, his arousal now limp. He took me in his arms, quite perplexed at my reaction.

"Oh, Charles I'm sorry, so sorry." I sobbed "I have ruined it for us."

"It's alright, darling. Just tell me what I did wrong. I thought you were enjoying everything."

"I was, I loved it. It, it was just when you rolled me over. It brought back bad, horrible memories."

He wanted to know. He did not want me to keep anything back. He did not want there to be any secrets between us. He held me in his arms and pulled up the sheet to cover my breasts. I ceased crying, took a deep breath, then related my sorry story: My father's molestation, the forced marriage to David, his abuse of me in that lodging house where he would force himself into my anus whenever he felt inclined, his fists bruising me and finally the punch which had caused me to miscarry. He usually managed to hit me where bruises did not show just as my father had hit mother. Then I told of that dank miserable room which always felt cold, of being short of money for the meter and also for food as David would drink away his meager earnings, how the surly landlady would poke her nose into the room, her eyes traveling to my swelling abdomen. "I hope you have not got a bun in the oven madam." She had admonished. "I have rules about that. I don't want my residents disturbed with all that crying and screaming, dirty nappies all over the place. If that's your situation, you will have to pack your bags." She did not have to wait long to evict us as soon after there was no baby to make a noise. I told him of the chipped shared basin on the first floor with the constantly dripping tap and of having to walk up two flights of creaking stairs to the rusty shared bath. I could not, however, bring myself to describe the state of it, the various shades of pubic hair clinging to the grey soap scum clogging the drain.

When I had finished my monologue, my sordid tale, I felt completely drained. Charles hugged me tighter and buried his face in my hair. He remained silent. It matched the stillness of the room, our room, our bridal suite. He turned towards me and took my face into his hands. I looked into his blue eyes dampened with tears and I was concerned how I now appeared with my blotchy face and red-rimmed eyes.

In a measured tone, he said, "My darling, darling girl. What you have been through I can scarcely imagine but remember this I would never ever hurt you. I will protect you until my last breath." "And," he added "I am so sorry for what happened just then. I thought it might have spiced things up a bit, that's all. I would not have done what that brute of a husband forced you to do."

Then I realized what he had been contemplating. It was the alternate of the missionary position.

"Oh, Charles. You must think I am so stupid and so naive, and me a midwife." I felt relieved then after the unburdening of my shocking secrets after all misunderstanding had been erased.

"Now," he said "What say we have a small glass of brandy to soothe us and then snuggle up for a good night's rest. It's been rather a big day in all respects don't you agree my angel?"

He located his underpants and put them on then climbed from the bed. He walked over to the cabinet and while he was pouring the brandy I quickly tried to neaten my hair with my fingers to make myself a bit more presentable but knowing it would be in vain. My face would still look a mess. He brought the balloons over and climbed into bed. We clinked glasses.

"I must look a fright," I pouted, "I would not blame you if you went back to that chapel and asked for a full refund."

"Never," he said but then stroking his chin thoughtfully added, "I take that back, maybe I should ask for half."

That brought a smile to my face as I playfully nudged his arm. I sipped the brandy and felt happy and relieved. Happy that I was married to this man who loved and who would protect me and relieved that it was him with whom I was able to share my terrible secrets.

Chapter Sixteen

"Good to see you back safe and sound your lordship, your ladyship," said Hudson inclining his head as Henry the footman dealt with our bags. The burning of a Jewish synagogue in Nuremberg and the threat of war with Germany had brought us back to Hagley Hall.

It had been a wondrous two months filled with sightseeing, laughter, and especially romance as we toured the great cities of Europe. Before departing the chateau, Charles had kept to his intention and taken us in the dinghy out on the moat. There was much laughter as I nearly upended us into the murky water as I scrambled to get on board.

"Look out!" cried Charles trying to steady the boat as it rocked from side to side. "I haven't been in one of these things before," I said as I managed to sit down on the wooden seat. "Now sit there and don't move," commanded my captain. "Aye, aye sir," I riposted giving him a salute as he put the gnarled oars into the water and rowed like the Oxford champion he was.

As we moved off I discerned our room high up in the tower and I thought of the languid morning we had spent making love and indulging in a room service breakfast of croissants aux chocolat and large mugs of milky coffee. I would always cherish the memories of our time in that tower room. Cherish how Charles had been so caring and empathic as I had relieved myself of those secrets I had kept hidden. It had been cathartic, the great weight I carried had been lifted and I was so grateful that he had been the person I had told, the one I loved the most.

From Rocamadour, we had motored through picturesque villages stopping at Lascaux to view the rock art then on to Sarlat where to my surprise we managed to locate Grandma's old house spilling with geraniums tucked away in a tiny street. I wished she could have still been there so I could tell her about our wedding in that holy chapel where she had taken her vows with Grandpa but I had to settle for thinking she would have looked down from heaven and given us her blessing.

In Paris we indulged in all the touristy activities, ascending the Eiffel Tower, marvelling at the Louvre, Notre Dame and Napoleon's Tomb. Charles had brought his box brownie camera and prevailed upon people to take our photos. Everyone had been most obliging as our loving gestures and embraces indicated we were honeymooners.

Auntie's warning about cheeky Italian men came to fruition, as my bottom had been pinched more than once as we strolled hand in hand along the streets of Rome.

"They can't resist such a belladonna," Charles had said to my complaints as another youth on a Vespa gave a wolf whistle in my direction. It was in the Sistine Chapel of St Peters Basilica that I felt most at peace and also in awe of the magnificence of the ceiling which Michelangelo had painted. We stayed there for a while sitting on the seat, holding hands, taking everything in.

Then we walked to the Basilica and knelt at one of the altars lighting candles, praying that Hitler would cease hostilities so that our future would be safe. The train had taken us then to Venice our accommodation being a 16th century Palazzo. Located near the Ponte de Cavallo it was where Charles had stayed a few years ago although he did not mention if Diana had been there with him and I did not like to ask him. After all, I thought as I looked from the balcony down to the gondolas plying the dark water, he had a past life as I had. It would not matter if the two of them had stayed here. I was here now with him and that was all that mattered. My wish of a gondola ride was granted after we had imbibed of Bellinis at Harry's Bar and dined al fresco on oysters and confit of duck courtesy of Hotel Monaco on the Grand Canal.

"Happy, my darling?" Charles asked. I snuggled deeper into his arms as the gondola took us under bridges and past the ancient palazzos of this magic city of water. I wondered what secrets would those houses reveal if those ancient walls could talk? The secrets of generations of people, people like us and particularly me navigating and dealing with the vicissitudes of life.

"Oh, yes, I am supremely happy," I whispered, our lips mingling. I breathed in his sweet smell, the woody cologne. It would always remind me of him. I was supremely happy and wanted this moment to continue. It was just us and the gondolier serenading us with Italian songs of romance, the moon our only source of light.

Our final day in Italy saw San Marco's Square teeming with the summer crowds. They were in competition with the multitude of pigeons that were fluttering and swooping on the crumbs of bread which people had left for them on the ground.

"It's so hot, darling," I said wiping my forehead with a handkerchief and shooing away a pigeon which had tried to land on my hat. I was pleased I had bought a few cotton dresses while in Rome and also some sandals which had wedge heels and which I thought rather smart.

"Do you want to have a cool drink?" asked Charles.

"Oh, yes please, that would hit the spot."

"I know just the place."

Taking my arm he escorted me through the pigeons to the other side of the square where a liveried waiter ushered us into Cafe Florian.

He seated us at a marble table near a window and with a flourish gave Charles a menu to peruse.

"Do you just want a drink or something to eat?" asked Charles

"Oh, I think a Limoncello, thanks, darling."

"Two Limoncellos por favor," said Charles to the waiter who, with nose in the air glided off with our order.

"He reminded me a bit of Hudson," I giggled.

"Yes, he did, now you mention it."

"I wonder how Hudson is," I mused as I fingered the silver sugar bowl "and everybody else," I added.

"I expect they are enjoying a bit of a break from routine, making the most of our absence," Charles replied.

"You know, I have not met your cook or our cook I should now say."

"Mrs. O'Hara?" I thought you had."

"No, we have never been introduced. I have only seen her fleetingly when I passed by the kitchen."

"Well, you will soon make her acquaintance when we return. You will be consulting her with menus and so on."

"Yes, I suppose that will be my duty as the lady of the house. I hope she will be more amenable than Mrs. Keen."

"Cook's a good old stick. I think you will like her although she does tend to get into a state when things are not functioning as she would like. I have heard that Rosie the scullery maid usually feels the lash of her tongue."

The waiter returned with a silver tray bearing our drinks. He set them down before us.

"And, as for Mrs. Keen, you should not let her bother you, darling." Charles said picking up his glass." I think she is a bit like your matron. Her bark is worse than her bite."

As we sipped our drinks, Charles told me that the cafe was the oldest in Venice and also the oldest operating cafe in the world. It had been the venue for many notable people, Dickens, Monet and Hemingway among others. It was certainly beautiful I mused as my eyes alighted on the frescoed ceiling, the paneled walls and marble tables and I wondered if any of these notable people had sat on the chairs on which we were sitting.

He paid the bill and refreshed, we returned to the madding crowds. To escape them and the heat we set off along the maze of alleyways through which the sun did not enter and discovered tiny workshops and an array of other shops selling all manner of items. We stopped at one, a jewelry shop, and through its window, I noticed items made of Murano glass. "Oh, look," I said pointing to a necklace of aquamarine, green and gold "Look at that one, isn't it lovely?"

He peered through the window.

"Come on," he said walking me through the door.

The assistant came over and Charles asked her to retrieve the necklace from the window.

It was more lovely when it was in my hand and even lovelier when the mirror revealed it fastened around my neck.

"Darling, thank you. It's just stunning. It will be a memento of our time here in Venice."

As the necklace was enfolded in layers of tissue paper and placed in a velvet box Charles, with a somewhat lascivious grin squeezed my waist and whispered in my ear.

"I hope that is not the only thing you will have as a memento." I knew what he was implying. Our Palazzo on the canal had borne witness to our unbridled passion as Charles had transported me to dizzying heights of ecstasy, had played me like a violin, teasing from me the notes I did not know I had possessed.

Now, we were back in the beautiful surrounds of Hagley Hall and were embarking on our journey as a married couple.

Chapter Seventeen

With Charles' support and also the indomitable Hudson I assumed the mantle of lady of the house without too much difficulty. Even Mrs. Keen's attitude towards me had improved and our relationship was more genial than when we had first met. My meekness had abated as my confidence grew and I felt more assertive in my dealings with her. I intuited that she had been used to Diana's rather domineering ways and strangely enough seemed to respect her for it. I wondered if she had any knowledge of Diana's lesbian relationship as housekeepers of these grand establishments seemed to be privy to their secrets. Maybe she had turned a blind eye like the three wise monkeys, hear no evil, see no evil, speak no evil. That would be Hudson's modus operandi, whatever a butler saw stayed with him never to be revealed. I rather enjoyed discussing menus with Mrs. Keen, taking her advice about the order of the courses, the color combinations and so on.

"It would be too brown, my lady," she advised when I had suggested the menu for the dinner party we were having for our friends after we returned from our honeymoon: beef, oxtail soup with a chocolate mousse to follow. She had advised me to settle on salmon, veal and a blackberry bavarois for dessert resulting in accolades from our guests who apart from the colonel were staying for the weekend. It had been more fun than the last time they had stayed as then I was only a fiance and was not yet the mistress of the house. This time the gramophone's volume was a little louder, the dancing continued until well after midnight and breakfast was whenever people felt inclined to eat. I think Hudson was glad when everyone departed for London and he could regain the usual routine which was what he was decidedly used to. However, to give him credit, he did not complain nor show any annoyance just continued to follow my orders and delegate to the rest of the staff.

๛๛๛

Charles' time was taken up with the overseeing of the estate, driving to his antique shop in London, calling on the tenant farmers and assessing any repairs to the house which required attention. He had been pleased that the dry rot problem had been fixed albeit at a cost as it had required a few roofers and there had been a delay due to inclement weather. However, it was not all work as time was found for us to motor to London spending nights at our pied a terre to attend the ballet at Covent

Garden and a Noel Coward comedy, Private Lives which was great fun.

It was on one of those nights that Bunny Williams made an altogether unseemly appearance. After not sighting him for a quite a length of time to our shock we had discovered him en flagrante delicto with a buxom peroxided siren naked in our bed, his only reply to Charles' admonishment was that he assumed it was ok for him to use the flat as he found it empty and he also had a key. I had been astounded that Charles had provided him with a key and insisted that Bunny hand it over and find himself somewhere else for his sexual activities. It had been the first disagreement Charles and I had since we met. I had looked forward to spending the night in our city flat. It would have been like a second honeymoon but like the linen Bunny and his floozy had cavorted in, all had been spoilt. Charles did his best to placate me even changing the sheets the sight of which eventually brought a smile to my face and all my consternation vanished as I thought of Hudson witnessing his lordship attempting to make a bed!

༄༅༄

It was late November as the clouds of war were becoming more portentous I knew to my joy I was expecting our child. However, the joy was tempered with concern that something would go awry, my womb could have sustained some lingering damage from the miscarriage

I had suffered as a result of David's assault. Charles did his best to reassure me that all would be well insisting that I consult professor Lambert, a prominent Harley Street obstetrician. I had intentions of delivering the baby here at the Hall with the assistance of a midwife but after much consideration and heeding Charles and the professor's advice booked in at Chelmsford Private Hospital in Aylesbury.

"I think you have made the correct decision your ladyship," advised Mrs. Keen when I had told her of my plan after discussing the menu for a forthcoming dinner we were to host. "One cannot be too careful when it comes to childbirth, even if you are a midwife."

All the staff had shown much happiness and wished us well when we had announced our news, Hudson sheepishly asking when the little one was due?

ജ‍ജ‍ജ‍

In a cloud of flour, Mrs. O'Hara had thrown down her pastry enfolding me in the confines of her ample bosom.

"Oh, your ladyship," she exclaimed, "that is the best news I have heard for many a day. A babby is what this house needs and no mistake."

"Can I play with it when it's bigger?" Rosie inquired from behind a mound of vegetables on the other side of the kitchen.

"You just concentrate on getting those potatoes peeled my girl," expostulated the cook who had now released me returning to the task of rolling out the pastry for an apple pie.

"You certainly will not have time for anything of the sort if I have anything to say on the matter. Playing with her ladyship's baby indeed! You will be the death of me girl, so you will."

Leaving Rosie to Cook's chastisement, I made my way out to the garden musing about what Charles had said that day in Florian. Cook was in control of her kitchen and was a hard taskmaster but underneath the bluster, she had a heart of gold and treated Rosie as she would her own daughter.

Standing by a wheelbarrow full of leaves I came across Charles in conversation with Mr. Mullins.

"How do your ladyship," he said doffing his battered cap. "I believe congratulations are in order. His lordship just told me your news."

"Oh, did he? Well, thank you Mr. Mullins," I replied taking Charles' hand.

"I think this calls for a little toast," said Mr. Mullins "That is if you both have time."

"I think we can spare a few minutes," replied Charles "don't you darling?"

"Yes, that would be lovely."

Our old gardener led the way across the grass and on to his tiny cottage at the edge of the wood. I had not known it was there hidden as it was behind a clump of trees.

"Here we are then," said Mullins opening the ivy-covered door. The ceiling was so low Charles had to duck his head as he entered the tiny room. On a colorful hearthrug, the cat was sprawled fast asleep. The small pine table was set with a cup, saucer and plate in readiness for the owner's supper and on the hutch in pride of place was a photo whom I surmised was of Mullins' late wife.

"Sit yourselves down," he commanded pointing to the aged settle squeezed into the corner of the room. It was obviously used as his bed as it was covered with a patchwork quilt under which a pillow protruded. From the cupboard, he withdrew three glasses and proceeded to pour a measure of whiskey into them. He brought the glasses over and sat down beside us.

"Well, here's health," he said downing the liquid in one swallow then helped himself to more. I looked across at Charles doing my best to stifle a giggle as I thought there would not be much more gardening undertaken if he continues at this rate.

"I hope your babby does not have the colic," he announced suddenly "I remember when our Alfie had it and the wife did not get much sleep for nigh on three months." I commiserated with him as I knew that colic was no fun either for baby or the parents.

"Your house is so cozy Mr. Mullins," I told him changing the subject putting my glass on the floor as there was nowhere else to place it.

"It does me and the cat just fine your ladyship. I would not know what to do with me self in anything bigger than this."

It was like a gingerbread house in a fairytale and could fit into one of the rooms at the Hall. We spent a few more minutes discussing Germany, Hitler and the possibility of a second war. As the sun was setting we left him to prepare his supper and probably finish off that bottle of whiskey.

My friends were also overjoyed at my news especially auntie Eil and I arranged to meet them all when I consulted professor Lambert in London. It took three attempts before I managed to contact Rachel. "I told you the date of our arrival Peggy," she had lambasted me through the telephone line as I had forgotten when she was returning from Berlin. "I don't know how you manage to run that grandiose mansion of yours if you cannot remember a simple thing as a date."

"Well," I bristled, "we cannot all be perfect. I was actually ringing to let you know you will be an aunt in August."

"Oh," she replied, "Well, I hope you don't expect me to travel to the wilds of Bedfordshire and babysit. As you know I'm not into the business of babies, all that crying and snotty noses and the mess they make."

She reminded me of that landlady in Brighton and I was tempted to tell her so, but I held my tongue. She was not aware of what I had endured there, and she never would. The conversation ended the way it always did leaving me feeling intimidated and upset and I determined that would be the final time I would vouchsafe to speak to her. She would always possess this officious attitude and would never bestow a kind word upon me. My health was all that mattered and the well-being of my baby so if severing ties with her was what it would take then so be it.

Aunt made up for Rachel's attitude when I called in to see her before lunching at a Lyons tea house with Audrey and Jean who were enraptured with the forthcoming birth due on 21st August under the star sign of Leo. I prayed the star would protect it especially from this war which was looming and which Neville Chamberlain believed could be stopped by appeasement. However, Churchill had a different view of the majority, his lone voice decrying all that the other politicians were espousing.

"What would you like, a boy or a girl?" asked Jean eyes aglow after we had ordered our sandwiches and a pot of tea.

"She would like anything as long as it is healthy," put in Audrey. "Isn't that right?"

I had to agree with her. After losing my other baby it was all that mattered. Just to give birth to a healthy full-term infant would be all that I would require. They both had known about my miscarriage but not its circumstances as I still possessed a shame about the whole event. It was only my beloved who knew and for the moment I wanted to keep it that way. Maybe one day

I would summon the nerve to tell them especially Audrey who was my best friend and who probably had a right to know. I felt a bit disloyal that I had not confided in her but time had gone on and with it my courage. I steered the conversation to matron who had recovered from her illness and back to her mordant self, then it was on to the patients and the hospital to which they would have to go as their lunch break was now coming to an end. With a promise to keep in touch we exchanged hugs and Bill then drove me to aunt's flat in Notting Hill.

"Oh, Peggy dear," she had said enveloping me in a hug and planting a wet kiss on my cheek "that is wonderful, I am so pleased for you both. Now you must take care of yourself especially after what you went through before." She was alluding to the miscarriage of which she had known although she also had not known it had been the result of David's fist.

"Yes, aunt I will," I replied. "Actually, I have just come from an appointment with an obstetrician in Harley Street. He thinks there should not be any problems."

"That is good dear," Aunt replied pouring more tea. "But I hope you don't suffer heartburn like your mother did with Rachel. I remember her saying it used to keep her up half the night."

I sipped my tea and thought that would be my sister, even the womb could not contain her venom leaching out making my mother suffer. I was on the verge of telling aunt about my phone call but thought better of it as it would have stirred up bad emotions and not serve any useful purpose.

"And how is that husband of yours?" she asked interrupting my thoughts.

"Oh, Charles is well. There is plenty to keep him busy. I did not realize how much work there is in overseeing an estate."

"But," I added, "How are you, and what have you been doing with yourself since the wedding, have you caught up with Cecily at all?"

She told me she had been in touch with her and they had been to a few exhibitions and charity functions. I was pleased they had become friends and shared some common interests. It did her good to be out and about taking her mind off her ailments especially sciatica which had always tended to bother her.

"Well, Aunt I'm afraid I shall have to love you and leave you," I said noticing the time as I finished off the last crumbs of cake.

"Oh, yes, dear, you don't want to leave it too late. It is quite a drive up there. It's a shame that chauffeur of yours could not have come in to have some cake and a cuppa with us."

I explained that Bill was used to waiting when driving us here and there and more often than not cook ensured that he had some provisions to sustain him like a thermos of tea and some doorstop sandwiches. She got up off the chair and escorted me to the door.

"You take care of yourself Peggy dear and thank you for dropping in to see me. It's so much nicer to see someone in person rather than talk on that telephone which I do not think I will ever get used to."

"Oh, you will aunt, it just takes time." I replied, "But I tend to agree. It is nicer to talk to someone face to face."

She gave me a hug and I left her waving frantically as Bill pulled away from the curb and whisked me back to Charles and the confines of my home at Hagley Hall.

Chapter Eighteen

The months ticked by dragging the world closer to war and it was on the 22nd August 1939 to my relief and joy after a twelve-hour labor, I was delivered of a healthy baby boy weighing eight pounds nine ounces. We named him James Andrew. With a tiny cleft in his chin and a mass of dark hair, he bore a striking resemblance to his father. Apart from indigestion and leg cramps in the latter stages the pregnancy had gone smoothly enabling us to entertain and host a few dinner parties the last one having been rather memorable as Charles had invited a few people from the Admiralty as well as Lord Beaverbrook and his mistress Jean. I had been briefed beforehand that he had been rather a lothario during his marriage, he ran The Daily Express and owned Cherkley Court on which the cream of society descended including Diana Cooper. He also enjoyed a good relationship with Churchill and was reputed to have met Hitler.

Mrs. O'Hara's culinary expertise had been put to the test devising the menu for this most significant occasion and she had indeed excelled as plates of pheasant, duck, salmon and other delicious comestibles were handed around by Hudson and the footman to the illustrious assembly. The conversation was about the war, the inevitability of it and the dining room resounded with opinions about confronting the might of the German Reich and Adolf Hitler. Military training had commenced in May the Government calling up all able-bodied men. Harold our groom and Henry the footman presented themselves for the obligatory medical examinations and both had passed the tests. I had been worried that Charles would be also prevailed upon but his weak chest mercifully had disqualified him from enlistment.

"It will be an ideological war," proffered the colonel "and the world will pay in blood."

"That may be so my good man," replied Beaverbrook, "but I cannot see we have much choice. That blighter Hitler is not to be trusted. He only knows one thing and that is to get his hands on as much territory as he can including this green and pleasant land!"

I sipped my wine and placed my other hand over my swelling belly in some futile attempt to protect my soon to be born infant, to keep him safe from this forthcoming tsunami of horror, a second world war which nobody wanted. I thought of the Great War, of my uncle, how he and many others like him from tiny villages and big towns all joined up to fight for King and country. How they spent years in the misery of rat-infested muddy trenches being pounded by cannons and poisoned by mustard gas, death being a happy release from the agony of their lives. Surely it would not be like that again. All those thousands of young men dying in their prime, some not even reaching their twenty-first birthday. Please God, I prayed as the discussion reverberated around the table, keep us all safe and let my baby grow up to celebrate all the milestones of his life. In bed that night as I was tossing and turning with my mind awash with concern we were alerted by a knock on the bedroom door.

"What the devil," said Charles who had been sleeping.

He rose from the bed and put on his gown then opened the door to Hudson also in his night attire.

"Beg pardon, your lordship but there is a telephone call for you from her ladyship's sister. She said it was a matter of extreme urgency."

"Very well, thank you, Hudson. I will be there presently."

I was now sitting up.

"What is she ringing you for at this hour?" I bristled.

"I don't know but I will soon find out. Go back to sleep."

He stepped into his slippers and padded downstairs leaving me to wonder what on earth was going on with Rachel. I had not contacted her since that day I told her I was pregnant nor had she contacted me. It would be just like her to ask for Charles and not me. She had not even spoken to him before. Why did she want to speak with him at this hour of the night?

My questions were soon answered when Charles returned. My sister and her lover were stuck in Berlin and as she knew that Charles had influence and friends in high places in the Government was pleading with him to use his power to get them back to Britain.

"What? Of all the cheek," I fumed. "They can jolly well stay there and suffer the consequences for all I care. She is really the limit, and I will bet she did not ask how I was or the baby who she could not care less about."

I went on seething with fury. How dare she ring up out of the blue expecting Charles to pull out all stops to save her from her own misadventure. She should not have gone over there in the first place.

"I hope you told her where to go," I fumed as I felt my heart racing with all the upset.

"I told her I would see what I could do but I would not promise anything. She certainly was in a state. She appeared to be in a telephone box in the street and there were sounds of breaking glass and lots of shouting."

I did not know what to think or feel when I heard that. Although she was certainly a bitch and had treated me appallingly, she was still my sister, my flesh and blood. I knew the situation in Germany was bound to be dire especially for the Jews. Why on earth did she go there in the first place with the war about to erupt? With Charles' arms around me, my heart resumed its normal pattern however sleep was fitful and my dreams were of Rachel being pursued by Swaztikas through the streets of Berlin. It was due to strings being pulled and Charles' influence in Government circles that a charter flight had been commandeered to bring my sister home. However, it was only she who could be rescued as Lucinda was not considered part of the bargain and she was left in Berlin to fend for herself. Naturally, this did not sit well with Rachel and she persisted harassing Charles who finally told Hudson and the staff not to put through any of her calls. The tactic worked. She soon tired of ringing as she knew she would not be able to speak to Charles and I knowing she was out of Germany resumed my previous attitude towards her. I would only speak to her if she wanted to speak to me.

Chapter Nineteen

Then what we had all been dreading came to fruition. As we all gathered around the wireless on 3rd September 1939 at 11:15 am Chamberlain broadcast the news that Britain was at war with Germany. Charles put his arm about my shoulder as I hugged little James even tighter to my bosom. Mrs. Keen bit her lip while Mrs. O'Hara complained about the inevitable food rationing and how was she going to make do with a quarter pound of meat per person per week.

Hudson said, "Well, that's that then." and promptly vacated the room to tend to his duties. It would take more than a war to disrupt his routine.

"It's a terrible to do," said Mullins and swiped at his eyes with his ragged handkerchief. Henry announced he would be joining up to be seconded by Harold mumbling he would join the navy sheepishly stealing a glance at Milly who appeared to look quite flushed. James began to wail as if he also knew of the cataclysm about to engulf us all. I carried him upstairs to the nursery and settling into the rocking chair put him to the breast. As he suckled noisily I felt so sad that this was all I could offer him, everything else was in God's hands. Charles came into the room with a cup of tea and a biscuit.

"Thought you could do with this darling," he said placing the tea on the small table beside me.

"Thank you, dearest, you are a brick," I replied putting James to the other breast.

"Should have put a slug of brandy in it," he added, "but we don't want our little one turning into an alcoholic."

That remark elicited a spark of humor from me and I was grateful. If we could both retain our humor it would be some sort of bulwark against the dark days which were ahead of us.

Charles went over to the window then turned to face me.

"Suppose I had better see about having the blackout curtains installed," he said.

"Oh, do you think we will have to have them?" I queried. "Surely the Germans won't be bombing us out here in the country?"

I knew that blackout curtains had been in place in London for a few months as the city would be the main target of the enemy.

"I hope they won't," Charles said. "but it is the law and it's better to be sure than sorry."

He came over and his lips brushed our heads before he made his way downstairs. There was nothing more to be said. We were both ensnared in our thoughts and concerns about the situation unable and unwilling to articulate them to each other. Now satiated James had fallen asleep. I carefully rose from the chair and placed him into his bassinette then covered him with the blanket. I stood for a few minutes just watching him, my precious baby oblivious to all that was occurring and would occur. Please God, I prayed, keep him and us safe here in this house and let this war be over quickly. Then I made my way downstairs to ring aunt and my friends who would obviously be more worried than I as they were in London right in the eye of the storm.

Chapter Twenty

As time passed the plans for the evacuation of children from London to the country swung into action and there were a few new little bodies scampering around the village.

Mostly from the east end they were not in possession of hygiene or manners.

"I had to put them into a bath and scrub them, your ladyship," the postmistress told me when we had met one morning on one of my outings with James. She had taken in two brothers aged six and seven.

"I don't know when they last had a proper bath," she whispered and warming to her theme added, "their hair was crawling with lice! And the language, it would put a sailor to shame."

As I listened my thoughts turned to my former patients, attempting to raise a brood of children with a drunken husband and hardly any income. These evacuees were the same, poor little mites, uprooted from their homes however humble and thrown into the houses of strangers. It was when I was pushing the pram back to the house an idea formed and I determined to broach it with Charles over supper.

"Well, if it's what you want darling," he said helping himself to the cheese platter which Henry had placed on the table.

"But it will be a lot to take on," he added. "You know what these children are like. I really think you should start considering employing a nanny to help you."

I had decided to foster one of the evacuated children and until now had managed James without the services of a nanny however what Charles had said about obtaining help made sense. The only assistance I had was from a local girl who soaked and washed the nappies pegging them on the line where they fluttered in the wind like little white flags.

"Yes, I suppose you are right. I shall contact the agency first thing tomorrow."

I placed my napkin on the table and flew around to my beloved. I enveloped him in a hug to thank him for agreeing to my plan just as Hudson entered the room.

"Beg pardon, your ladyship, your lordship," he sheepishly said. "Would you be requiring anything else?"

"No, that will be all thank you, Hudson," replied Charles as I straightened up and returned to my seat resuming the dignity of the lady of the house.

The thought of caring for one of those children was uppermost in my mind that night as I lay in bed the snores of Charles adding to my restlessness. It was a relief when the room was lightened by the thin rays of the sun and I could put my plans into action. The first call I made was to the employment agency who advised they had a couple of good candidates who were willing and ready to travel here today to be interviewed for the position.

The second call was to the organization responsible for the placement of the child evacuees.

"Yes, madam," said Mrs. Halloran. "We do have a few boys who are still in need of homes. Around what age were you contemplating?"

I had not really thought about it but suddenly decided on a five-year-old. He would hopefully be toilet-trained and ready to attend the village school. Arrangements were put in place and I was informed that he would arrive within the next couple of days.

In the afternoon while Charles had gone to visit the colonel I stood by the window in the library, cigarette in hand awaiting the arrival of two prospective nannies. My eyes alighted on the garden, in particular, the bush from which I had cut the roses for Diana's grave. It all seemed so long ago, the funeral, our engagement, and now here I was the mistress of Hagley Hall with a baby son and soon to protect another child from the bombs of this dastardly war. I wondered about Diana's lover, where she was and if she was involved with someone else. Was she in London or somewhere in Germany? My thoughts then turned to my sister, how was she faring without the company of Lucinda? Had she become involved with someone else? A knock on the door brought me back from my reveries.

"Pardon me your ladyship," announced Hudson. "There is a Miss Perkins here to see you."

"Thank you, Hudson, you may show her in."

A vision in red with lips to match and topped with blond corkscrew curls wiggled through the door and it was not long until she was on her way out. Although she possessed the right qualifications her attitude was too flirtatious and during the interview I had caught her more than once peering through the window trying to attract the attention of Bill who was polishing the car. The next candidate was just the opposite. Miss McKay presented as a mature Scottish woman, grey hair pulled back severely into a bun and a face devoid of makeup. She had been in the employ of a Lady Pemberton in Aberdeen caring for her three children. Her reference attested she had been a capable and trustworthy employee and had left the position as her employer had moved to the United States.

"Oh aye, I find the boys require more discipline than the girls," she said after she had been informed about James and the other boy I was intending to foster. We chatted for a while longer which led me offering her the position which she accepted with alacrity. It was agreed that she would commence the following day.

"Well, I hope she works out then," said Charles that evening. We were in the library enjoying a brandy after it had taken quite a time to settle little James. I hoped he was not sickening for something but his forehead was cool and he did not have a fever. Charles had told me I was being overprotective, running to his cot making sure he was covered and his breathing was normal and feeding him whenever he whimpered. It was probably due to the fact that I had lost my first child and could not bear to lose another. Maybe when the nanny came I would be more reassured and having the other boy might make a difference.

"The other one did sound like a bit of a flibberty gibbet," he continued, "the way you described her. Poor Bill would not have stood a chance!" It had been rather comedic I thought as I sipped my brandy and snuggled closer to Charles the coals in the grate suffusing the room with a warming glow. She reminded me of that blond we had caught with Bunny that night in our pied a terre.

I asked Charles.

"I wonder what Bunny is up to these days. It has been a while since you have seen him."

"Oh, yes, I meant to tell you, darling. It must have slipped my mind. Apparently, he enlisted and has been training at a barracks in Chatham in Kent."

That might knock some sense into him I mused. A taste of army discipline might be just what he needs. In companionable silence each with our own thoughts, we stayed until the coals had burnt down and the grandfather clock struck twelve reminding us it was time to retire for the night. Charles went on ahead while I poked my head around the door of the nursery for a final check and discovered thankfully that my little one was sleeping peacefully.

⍟⍟⍟

"Pardon me, your ladyship, Miss McKay has arrived," said Hudson the following morning as the clock struck eleven. I was in the library sorting through some old Tatler and Country Life magazines. Charles had gone to see about obtaining more pigs to add to our Berkshire litter.

"Show her into the drawing room, Hudson. I will be there shortly."

I put down a Tatler, smoothed my hair and straightened my skirt thinking if nothing else at least she is punctual.

"Good morning Miss McKay," I said extending my hand which she took in a firm grip.

"Good morning your ladyship but you can call me nanny Mack. It is what I am used to."

"Well, Nanny Mack it is then."

Summoning Hudson who dealt with the luggage I showed her to her room then took her to the nursery where James was awake and demanding to be free of his cot.

I picked him up and handed him to her.

"Oh, he is a bonny bairn," she said chucking him under the chin to which he responded with a chuckle.

"Yes," I replied, "he is usually a happy little soul except when his hunger turns him into a male virago."

She tutted at this, indicating her displeasure giving me the impression that he should not be fed whenever he was upset

I reminded her of our foster child whose arrival was due tomorrow and expressed concern that he might prove more than she could handle.

"Don't you worry your ladyship," she said drawing herself up to her full height, "no child has ever got the better of me. Now, how about I take this one for a nice walk in the fresh air while the day is still fine?"

"Oh, yes. That is a good idea."

We trooped downstairs passing Milly who was polishing the banisters and I noticed she looked rather peaky.

"Milly, this is nanny Mack. Would you please show her where the perambulator is kept?"

"Pleased to meet you I'm sure," said Milly putting down her duster and tin of polish

"And you Milly," replied nanny.

I decided to come with them, to make sure James was well covered with his blankets as while it was sunny there would still be a chill in the air.

As I watched her depart with James I felt a kind of sadness. It was always me who took my baby for his walks, pushing the pram along the country lanes, talking to him about the birds in the trees and anything else we encountered. Now it seemed I would relinquish control, it would be the nanny who would assume that role and I would be taking a back seat. However, he would still need me for his feeds which I intended to continue if my milk supply held. Up until now, there had not been any problems in that department and I loved the bond which had formed while nursing. I felt fortunate that I had not experienced the discomforts which my patients had to endure; the cracked nipples and the mastitis which poor Mrs. Watts had suffered. I made my way back to the house thinking about that new child who would be here tomorrow and undoubtedly be in need of care and attention.

"I just this minute had a telephone call from his lordship," said Hudson greeting me in the hall.

"Apparently, he decided to stop off and see the colonel and will not be here for luncheon. Would madam prefer to eat on the terrace as it is such a lovely day?"

It was a lovely day and the terrace was just the place to take full advantage of it.

"Yes, thank you, Hudson I would enjoy that."

"Very well, I will see to it. Mrs. O'Hara advised that is a cold collation. Would madam prefer a glass of white wine as well?"

I requested a glass of chilled Moselle. That and the sun would be just what I needed and hopefully help to dispel the melancholy I was still feeling. It was probably a lot to do with the war. It was making everyone tense and less cheerful I told myself as I sat with my plate of cold meat and salad. I sipped my wine and wished Charles was here to share this time with me and not with the colonel. Time was short now the war had begun and we had to make the most of every minute. But I knew he had matters to attend to concerning the estate and could not be expected to accompany me during the day. It was the husbands who worked and the wives who stayed home just as my mother had. At least my husband was here with me at night and not propping up some bar as my father had done. I sat back and closed my eyes letting the sun warm my face. I must have dozed off for a few minutes when I noticed my watch said it was two fifteen. My god, two fifteen! Where was nanny and little James? They should have been back ages ago. I started to panic. Something must have happened and James would be overdue for his feed. Just as I leaped off the chair to raise the alarm I heard the scrunch of gravel and the cries of James.

"Where have you been?" I demanded as I flew down the steps visions of them lost in the maze now receding from my mind.

"Och, no need to worry madam, we were with your old gardener. Nice little nook he has there. He is a character, said I could call in any time for a chin wag."

"That is not appropriate, nanny," I admonished detecting an aroma of alcohol wafting about her. She had clearly been tippling with Mullins "You are here to look after the children not gossiping with the staff. I thought you might have got lost in the maze or something worse."

Now James' wails were louder. I angrily scooped him up from the pram and raced inside to feed him leaving nanny on the gravel to contemplate her misbehavior.

Chapter Twenty-One

"Want to do a wee!" yelled young Mervyn whose face was one only a mother could love and his elephant ears did nothing to enhance his appearance. He had just arrived with Mr. Plummer, his escort on the eleven-ten train from Paddington. Nanny, eyebrows raised, had quickly hustled him out to the guest bathroom as Hudson poured the tea. I had been keeping an eye on her since that transgression with Mullins. In Mervyn's absence, I asked Mr. Plummer how the child was coping having being torn asunder from his family and also about his behavior during the train journey.

"He had been quiet for the most part m'lady," he replied, "but to tell the truth he certainly could do with a good soak in a hot bath with plenty of carbolic soap." I was reminded about the postmistress' charges and hoped there would not be any unwelcome guests in his hair! If that was the case nanny was going to have her work cut out. The conversation was about the situation in London with Mr. Plummer apprising us just how horrific it was. He told us of the constant air raids, the people sleeping end to end in the underground stations to escape the onslaught of Hitler's bombs, and the incongruity of a kitchen sink or lavatory standing intact amongst the rubble of the houses in which they had resided. He was brought to tears about what he had seen yesterday. It was a woman. her clothes blown off by the force of a bomb. With glazed eyes, she had been standing amidst the rubble of her house, her dead baby beside her. It was terrible to hear and I was grateful that we were in the peace of the countryside away from the nightmare which was unfolding. I found myself praying that aunt, Cecily, and my friends would be safe as they were in London in the line of fire and, although Rachel and I were estranged, my hope was the bombs would not travel as far as Cambridge.

"Your ladyship," commented nanny after giving Mervyn a good scrub in the bath.

"I have never encountered such a dirty child. The water was nearly black. I don't know when he had his last wash and his hair! I will have to take kerosene to it. He has the lice. I wouldn't let him get too close to the babby."

I commiserated with her even offering my services at which she, of course, had scoffed.

"Your ladyship cannot be involved in such unseemly duties." she had said hauling poor Mervyn out to the scullery from which emanated cries of disgust from Mrs. Keen and cook to be followed by the cries of poor Mervyn as the chemical was poured over his head.

He had by now been scrubbed within an inch of his life and deloused and I had located him in the room he had been allocated. Dressed in a pair of pajamas which obviously were hand-me-downs, much too big and frayed around the edges he sat on the floor with downcast eyes.

"Hello pet," I said as I knelt on the floor beside him.

Pulling at a loose thread in the rug he eyed me suspiciously and said "Are you my mam now?"

"Yes, darling," I replied taking his little hand and noticing his nails which were bitten to the quick.

"I am but only for a while. We are going to keep you safe here in this big house in the country."

"Did you bring any toys or books to read?"

"Don't have no toys or books," he replied disconsolately still worrying the thread.

"Well, what about tomorrow we go to the village and buy something for you? Would you like that?"

"All right but I ain't got no money."

"You don't need any money, darling. I will buy you whatever you need. Would that be good?"

He thought for a moment then nodded.

"And," I added, "Would you like to see our pigs on our way back from the village?"

His little face lit up.

"I love piggies, he said enthusiastically.

"Can we see 'em now?"

"No, pet, not now. It is rather late."

"What color are they?" he asked. I had at last piqued his interest and drawn him out of his disconsolation.

"They are black pigs called Berkshires."

"I saw a brown pig one day," he offered.

"Did you sweetheart. Where did you see it?"

"It was when my da took me to a farm."

"Did you enjoy going there?"

"Yer, I liked it."

Aware of the time I suggested that we go down and see what was for dinner. He scrambled up off the floor and holding my hand we went downstairs to the kitchen where some rabbit pie and a glass of milk awaited.

"Now, go easy laddie," admonished Nanny as he shoveled the food into his mouth as though he had not eaten in weeks. "We don't want you sick on your first night here."

Nanny asked,

"Do you want me to give the babby his bottle tonight your ladyship?"

"No, thank you, nanny, I shall do it. I will come to say goodnight to Mervyn when you have put him to bed," I replied as I ruffled his hair which still contained the odor of kerosene but at least it was devoid of creatures.

"Very well, your ladyship and I dare say it won't be long until the laddie will be asleep. It has been a long day for him."

"Yes," I replied, "it has been a long day for everyone." I walked over and took James' bottle from the saucepan in which it had been heating leaving Mervyn to finish his supper under nanny's hopefully watchful eye.

In bed that night I discussed the day's events with Charles but was careful not to mention the lice in Mervyn's hair. I thought it might make him regret his agreement to foster this child and he would be concerned that James might contract some sort of disease.

"I think there might be a few old toys in the attic," he said after I told him about Mervyn's lack of entertainment.

"I will ask Hudson to look for them tomorrow."

"Thanks, darling. That would be wonderful. I feel so sorry for the poor pet."

With my arm around Charles, we snuggled under the blankets and had not been asleep for long when we were alerted by loud screams.

"What on earth?" Charles said sitting up.

"It must be Mervyn. Stay there and I will go," I replied hastily donning my gown leaving Charles to resume sleeping.

I raced along the corridor to Mervyn's room where I found him sitting up in bed his face streaked with tears.

"Shush now, pet. It's all right now. You were just having a bad dream."

I put my arms around him and felt his little heart racing.

I rocked him and with soothing words managed to settle him down. I wondered where nanny was. Why she was not here. She must have heard his cries. Then the cries of James rent the air. I ran to the nursery where James was standing bawling in his cot. Picking him up I gave him his dummy which I found tangled in the sheets and after he was settled I staggered back to bed where Charles was sleeping soundly.

ഇഇഇ

It was in the morning I encountered nanny making a pot of tea in the kitchen.

"Did you sleep well your ladyship?" she enquired sitting herself down and adding three teaspoons of sugar to her cup.

"No, as a matter of fact, I did not nanny," I replied standing before her and not sitting down as I needed to assume an authoritative stance.

"Oh, why was that m'lady?"

"Because nanny, I was up half the night with the children. Mervyn had a terrible nightmare that woke James. I expect you to fulfill your duties and be at the children's bedside whenever they are upset."

She seemed rather nonplussed at my admonishment however had offered an apology assuring me it would not happen again. I left her agreeing to have the children ready in two hours for an expedition into the village.

ഇഇഇ

The day was pregnant with promise, as we set off along the lane Mervyn's animation and excitement erasing the terror of the previous night. However the thought of nanny's bleary eyes this morning took the edge off my content. Father had presented in such a state after he had had his fill of drink making my suspicions of nanny's behavior even stronger. I determined one way or the other to ascertain if my intuition was correct.

"Can I 'ave these?" asked Mervyn clutching some dog-eared comics to his chest. We had arrived at the village jumble sale where Mervyn had spotted a collection of comics on one of the stalls.

"Yes, pet, If you will enjoy them," I replied thinking as I handed over the money at least he can look at the pictures even if he cannot read. I must talk to Charles and see about enrolling him at the local school at which the other evacuees attended. Happy with his purchase and while James was sleeping I thought I would take him to see the old church. It was as I had found it the last time I was here, dark, musty, the aroma of candlewax in the air. We sat in one of the pews, the only other visitor an aged lady her bescarfed head bowed in prayer at the foot of the altar. I pointed out to Mervyn the stained-glass window. He surprisingly seemed quite interested that it was the same design as the chapel at the house where he now lived. He asked me about the bible scenes and what they all signified and I had the impression that his intelligence was not to be underrated. We walked over to where the candles burned and I gave him one to light for the war to end and to keep us all from harm.

The tea shop was our next stop as James was due for his feed. We sat at the same table at which I had sat the first time I visited. While I gave James his bottle and Mervyn devoured a large slice of flourless cake in record time, his precious comics beside him, I mused how different everything was, how much water had flowed under the bridge since that first day I had walked to this village, how in a time of peace fate had contrived to bring Charles and me together. Now we were plunged into the dark of war and I had two children to care for and protect, albeit one for a little while. I mused what Rachel would think of poor Mervyn and could envision her reaction. She was averse enough to children let alone one who was from the east end, dirty and uncultured to say nothing of his hair full of nits. It brought a smirk to my face and I was tempted to turn up on her doorstep unannounced with Mervyn and wailing James in tow to see her reaction.

"Good day, your ladyship," said Mrs. Hannon who was entering the shop just as were exiting.

"Is this your young man?" She was assessing Mervyn who looked as though he wanted to be on his way itching to look at the comics clutched to his chest.

"Yes, I replied. "This is Mervyn. Say hello to Mrs. Hannon, pet. She is looking after a little boy from London just like you."

His eyes traveled shyly towards her and he mumbled something resembling a greeting.

"I think he is a little overwhelmed at the moment, Mrs. Hannon." Pointing to the comics I added, "And I think he is dying to get home to look at these."

Laughing, she replied, "I think you may be right your ladyship. I know my boy is the same. Has his nose in the comics whenever he can. Will Mervyn be attending school?"

"Yes, we hope to enroll him. Has your boy settled in?"

"Yes, he has now but it took a little while. But what can you expect when their world has been turned upside down by this wretched war."

James wailed and as I had promised Mervyn we would stop to look at the pigs, I politely ended the conversation and we commenced our journey home.

I broached the subject of school and there was no enthusiasm shown even when I indicated there would other children with whom he could befriend and play. He kicked a stone with his shoe which I noticed was in need of a new sole then changing the subject asked how long it would be before he saw the pigs and if he could play with the dogs when we arrived home.

"It's not much further," I replied thinking that it would not be the end of the world if he missed out on some schooling. Perhaps I and nanny could maybe teach him for the short while he would be with us and the way everything was at the moment. School was not really a priority.

"I can see them," he shouted as the pen came into view.

He ran off as fast as his little legs could carry him and it was an effort for me with the pram to keep up.

"Don't go into the pen," I shouted knowing that it was full of mud but my warning had fallen on deaf ears as he leaped over the fence and straight into the quagmire the pigs squealing and grunting at their unwelcome trespasser.

He was covered in mud from head to foot and was having the time of his life. A little dirt would not hurt him I thought, after all, it could be washed off. It was better that he could garner whatever enjoyment he could while he could as who knew what was to befall us all in the dark days ahead.

Nanny was most displeased at the state of him and it was in a flash that a bath was drawn. His protestations ignored, he was plunged in as another cake of carbolic soap was wielded and the washcloth flayed around his ears. While he was being scrubbed I took James into the library and set him down on the rug. He was always fascinated by the fire burning in the grate and had to be watched carefully as he was starting to crawl.

As I lit a cigarette Hudson entered and asked if I would like a cup of tea.

"Oh yes, I would rather, thank you, Hudson. Has his lordship returned?"

Charles had gone to a community meeting to discuss contingency plans if the enemy found their way here.

"No, my lady I'm afraid he has not returned as yet."

I knew these meetings often went overtime with the attendees all keen to put their views across.

He started to retreat but seeming to have an afterthought came over to the chaise.

"Yes, Hudson?" I said leaping up to pull James back from the fire. I sat him on my lap out of harm's way where he proceeded to pull at my hair.

"Well, your ladyship," he continued, "I have a rather delicate matter I wish to discuss with you and now seems an opportune time while there is nobody about."

I wondered what he wanted to discuss.

"Very well, Hudson I am all ears."

"Well, your ladyship," he said again conspiratorially leaning towards me as though there were people in the room.

"It seems that nanny has a problem."

"What problem Hudson?"

"A problem with the drink your ladyship."

My suspicions had been confirmed. That accounted for the bleary eyes, the nonattendance at night when the children were upset, the socializing with Mullins.

"Do you have any evidence, Hudson?" I asked.

"I have noticed the level in the sherry decanter has been down in the morning," he replied, "and as you and his lordship do not partake of the spirit I knew it would not have been you. Also, it pains me to say I have detected rather an alcoholic odor about her during the day and have noticed some trembling of the hands-on one or two occasions. An uncle of mine had the same symptoms and he died of cirrhosis of the liver."

I thanked him for apprising me of the situation and said I would deal with the matter and he retreated from the room to fetch my tea.

She would have to go I thought as James' trusting little blue eyes looked into mine. There was no way she could continue to look after the children. I thought about the reference she had proferred. It had probably been written by her. She had probably been dismissed from her previous employment. I berated myself for being so gullible and jejune. But what was done was done and I determined to set a trap and catch her in the perpetration of her crime.

છ૦છ૦છ૦

That night, after all had retired and Charles was asleep, I crept downstairs. Ensuring the decanter was full I hid behind the dining room door waiting for the culprit to materialize. It did not take long as nanny in nightgown and nightcap padded into the room heading straight to the decanter on the sideboard. I sprang from my hiding place.

"Oh, oh, your ladyship," she shouted spilling the sherry in her astonishment.

"What, what are you doing here?"

"More to the point, nanny what are you doing? Helping yourself to the sherry in the middle of the night," I countered.

"Oh, well, you see I couldn't sleep and I thought a nip of sherry would help me get off. Purely medicinal, I assure you."

I squared my shoulders and said censoriously.

"I don't think so, nanny. Mr. Hudson has told me about the dwindling supply of sherry and I think it is you who have been helping yourself as you are now doing. I have had my suspicions about your behavior and I do not want you looking after the children any longer. I am sorry, but you leave me with no choice but to terminate your services forthwith. I shall pay you up to the end of the month. Please have your bags packed tomorrow morning and Bill will drive you to the station."

"Aye," she mumbled slinking off to her room leaving me quite unsettled about the whole episode as it was not in my nature to be involved in a confrontation. However, I had enough alcoholism tainting my life and the safety of the children was paramount. It was this which had driven my belligerence. It was with a somewhat heavy heart I made my way back to bed, to Charles who was snoring loudly, oblivious of the contretemps which had just occurred in the dining room downstairs.

The next morning I told him about what had transpired and he had agreed with me that the safety of the children was all that mattered but I should have been more careful in verifying her reference. Mervyn was unconcerned about her absence probably relishing the thought of no more carbolic scrubs and kerosene shampoos and little James was too young to notice.

Hudson was pleased that all had been resolved as he could not abide by anything untoward taking place on his watch. Mrs. Keen had opined that she had thought there was something about nanny Mack she could not abide and seemed pleased that her authority in the house had returned to being unchallenged.

🕸🕸🕸

Mullins seemed rather disconsolate when I encountered him in the garden the day after nanny's departure.

"She just went without a by your leave, your ladyship. I didn't know she was going. You would think she would have said goodbye after all the good times we had."

He continued, "She could put away that whiskey and no mistake. I reckon she could drink me under the table if she had half a chance!"

I had been taken aback by this. The problem had been worse than I had thought and I felt vindicated about my decision to sack her.

An advertisement was placed for another nanny however after many interviews none was found to be suitable. I decided to continue with Mary the girl from the village and accepted the assistance of Mrs. Keen. I perceived she would prefer to lend a hand rather than have some other nanny usurping her authority. After some cajolement and bribes, Mervyn was now attending school so it was just little James to be cared for throughout the day. It was with renewed pleasure that I resumed pushing him in the pram into the village and taking Mervyn home after school had finished.

Chapter Twenty-Two

The war raged on during the months that followed. The newspapers and the wireless reported that London had been hit by high explosive and incendiary bombs continuously for 57 days. The docks had been targeted and other parts of Britain such as Liverpool and Manchester had also suffered from Hitler's savagery. The mention of Manchester brought to mind Bunny Williams and I wondered how many Germans he had shot. With his gung-ho attitude, I imagined he would be giving the Germans a good taste of their own medicine. Although I could not forget how he had misbehaved towards me I was surprised that I could not help but cheer him on. Perhaps it was the war. Everything took on a different perspective nobody knowing if they would live or die. I had surmised that had been the case when Milly had presented herself to me one morning in the library. My instincts had been correct when with now a noticeable belly she had divulged that, "I am in the family way, your ladyship," immediately bursting into tears. "It was only the once I laid with him," she said; him being Harold the groom who was presently somewhere on the high seas in the Atlantic unaware of his impending fatherhood. It had been sadness I had felt for her as I knew how easy it was for naive girls to be taken in as I had been. However, she left me no choice but to accept her resignation.

With a reference and two month's wages, she had returned home to her mother who I hoped would be supportive but knowing in my heart she would not. She lived in a tiny village whose inhabitants' tongues would be clicking when they caught sight of the pregnant hussy in their midst. However, I was overjoyed to hear from aunt who had accepted Cecily's offer to move in with her as the bombing became more intense. She had recounted that at the first sign of a siren, the two of them would flee to the Anderson shelter in Cecily's back garden, comforting themselves with copious amounts of thermos tea liberally laced with brandy while drowning out the noise of the bombs overhead with renditions of songs from Gilbert & Sullivan operettas.

⁊⁊⁊

The children were growing up; Mervyn forging a close bond with his baby brother. Apart from rousing on him when he upset the marble games at which Mervyn played with a friend in his room after school, he tolerated his baby ways in rather a mature fashion.

Since the day he was brought here to us, I had become attached to him, looking upon him as my child, nursing him through fevers and chickenpox, teaching him to treat others as he would wish to be treated. He had been so excited when we organized a fair on the grounds inviting all his friends from school and the people from the village. There had been egg and spoon races, elephant shy and tombola and even a clown under whose costume lurked the publican of the White Hart hotel.

"That was the best day ever mam," he had told me when I was tucking him into bed, "It was like Christmas."

He was referring to the last Christmas he had spent here at Hagley Hall, the giant decorated tree under which was a plethora of gaily wrapped presents a few of which were for him, the Christmas lunch where crackers were pulled and afterward charades were played. He had whispered he had never had a Christmas like this at home. Christmas had been like any other day, scavenging for lumps of coal to keep the fire going, his mother rewarming the pot of soup which was always on the hob yelling at his siblings to keep the noise down as his father sunk in the scraggy chair recovering from Christmas Eve's libations at the pub.

೮೨೮೨೮೨

It had been a few weeks after the fair that Mervyn's mother had telephoned, her message sending waves of perturbation through me.

"Me and Alfie need our Mervy back home and sooner the better," she squawked, "There's no one to run the messages. Alfie works long hours and I got a crook leg from one of 'em bombs that bloomin' Hitler sent over. I can't be walkin' all the way to the shops and all the other kids are too young to go."

She continued on as I visualized what poor Mervyn would be returning to. Treated like a skivvy and thrown into the cataclysm which was engulfing London but she was his mother and had priority over him. Who was I to deny her the right to reclaim her child? With a heavy heart, I acceded to her request and agreed to take him to London the day after tomorrow on the train. Charles' disappointment was pronounced when I had told him Mervyn would be leaving us in two days' time. Although he did not articulate his concerns about the dangers Mervyn would face in London, I knew by the tell-tale way he was rubbing his eyebrow that he was as worried as I.

We had told him in his room amongst the train set which Charles had unearthed in the attic, among the tin soldiers, the comics bought with the pocket money Charles had bestowed on him for the odd chores he undertook around the house, collecting the eggs and the newspaper from the delivery boy, as well as helping Hudson polish the silver as, according to him, even though there was a war and we had next to no staff, standards still had to be kept. The poor child seemed to take the news in good spirits, the only concern he had was that the school should be notified of his absence. He was doing well with his studies, his writing had improved and also his reading which I encouraged by reading books to him and James before lights out. Perhaps he thought he was going home until his mother recovered and he would return to us and resume his schooling. We could not bring ourselves to tell him otherwise. Better that he went with some sort of hope in his heart.

It was a restless night as I lay awake envious of Charles' snores. Why do men snore I wondered and how was it they were not as perturbed about matters relating to their children as mothers were? Perhaps I concluded as dawn broke it was because women were the givers of life, the nurturers and it behove us to go to our children's aid whether it was day or night.

ཀྲཀྲཀྲ

As I walked him to school knowing it would be the final day of doing so I determined to put on a brave face and not let him see the distress which was threatening to burst forth from me at any moment and it was with relief when I left him to scamper off in the playground with his classmates around him.

The headmaster had been as disappointed and surprised as us. "I am sorry to hear that your ladyship," he said, "the lad was settling in nicely and was showing some potential. Let's hope he can continue with his studies in London." But we both knew that would not eventuate and his future, if he was to have one, would be bleak.

Chapter Twenty - Three

I had taken him on the train which had been rather a challenge, squeezing through a jumble of kit bags and flirtatious smoking soldiers all enjoining us to sit with them as the train jolted and plodded on towards our destination. Amongst the soldiers and harried people on the platform I had spotted her, a dumpy woman in a threadbare coat too tight, hair awry waddling towards us,

"Oh, Mervy," she said grabbing him and slobbering kisses on his cheek, "I 'ave missed you and how you've grown, you are a big boy and no mistake." She had then seized the basket which he had been carrying and peered inside. "What 'ave we here eh?"

For the journey cook had made some spam sandwiches, slices of flourless cake, two apples and a bottle of lemonade however we both lost our appetites and had not touched the food. There was also a marble which little James had thrown in determined to give his big brother a farewell present.

"It's what cook gave me mam," Mervyn explained.

"Well," she shouted, "mustn't let good food go to waste. We can have this for our tea, better than the bread and dripping we were goin' to have. And..." she added, "What's this?" unearthing the colored glass ball which had settled into the bottom of the basket. Mervyn started to respond but his voice was drowned out by the bellow of an engine.

With a cursory thank you from her and a wave from Mervyn, my cheeks sodden with unchecked tears I watched them depart, caught up in the frenzied vortex of the station.

With leaden heart, I had returned to Charles and my baby and it was only a couple of days that our lives were soon turned upside down as the Hall had been requisitioned for the recuperation of soldiers suffering from shell shock and other injuries. We had received a formal notice from the government a few weeks previously, Charles and the colonel advising me that the Hall had been requisitioned in the last war as had other large estates including Highclere Castle in Hampshire.

The army duly arrived with beds and blankets and the dining room soon resembled a ward in a hospital. It had been all hands on deck as everyone pitched in to reorganize the rooms to accommodate the patients. The government compensated us for the soldier's upkeep, for their food and any other requirements. Cook had been pleased about that as she was already at her wits' end trying to keep us reasonably fed on the rations allocated to us. Bill had been prevailed upon to lend a hand. His flat feet had precluded him from enlisting so he was put to work helping lift the soldiers in and out of bed and running errands into the village. Petrol had been rationed so there were no long journeys undertaken.

ଈଔଈଔ

The books in the library were put into circulation, the patients who could manage to read devouring them with avarice. The others who had been rendered blind I would read to sometimes with little James on my lap. His baby talk seemed to have a calming influence and I surmised it might have reminded them of home and perhaps the families they had left behind. I also wrote letters for their loved ones, their dictated words always bringing a tear to my eye and I thought how fortunate Charles and I were to be here in the safety of our home away from the carnage and misery of this terrible war. Charles did his bit. Popping in to chat with the ones who wished to talk, trying to assure them that hopefully, the war would soon be over, they would regain their health and return to their families.

"Nurse," a soldier called out as I was entering the room with an armful of sheets having just put James down for his afternoon nap.

I hurried over to his bed.

"I can feel pain in my leg but I do not have a leg, do I?" he asked pointing to the stump where his leg had been.

"No, I answered. "I'm afraid you haven't. You have what is known as phantom pain where the brain is tricked into thinking the limb is still there."

He told me his name was Peter and took on board what I had told him albeit thinking it all rather strange and then asked me if I could bring him another book to read. I went to the library and brought him back The Great Gatsby.

"Oh, I say that is splendid," he said taking the book from me. "Thanks ever so."

"I wonder," he added, "if there are any equestrian books for Charlie over there." He pointed to a sleeping form near the window.

"You see he told me he rather enjoyed riding before the war."

"As a matter of fact, I do," I replied thinking what a nice fellow he was thinking of someone else.

"There are some old copies of Horse & Hound which I think he should like. I will look for them when I have changed the sheets.

"Thanks," he replied, "That should buck him up a bit."

Charlie had come to us in rather a bad way. He was terribly disfigured losing part of his face due to a gunshot wound. He usually remained cheerful, raising the spirits of all with his jokes and renditions of the latest songs such as "Hang out your washing on the Siegfried Line."

This would be followed by howls of, "Don't give up your day job Charlie and, "put a sock in it!"

ೕೕೕ

So, it was with a sense of foreboding when I was changing the flowers in the hall the following day I realized not much noise emanating from the dining room.

I went in. Everyone was quiet.

I walked over to Peter.

"Is everything all right?" I asked him. "Only I have not heard Charlie's dulcet tones this morning."

I was saddened to hear that Charlie had received a Dear John letter. His fiancé had broken off their engagement after visiting him one day. I noticed she had fled into a waiting cab after only a few minutes by his side. He had taken the news badly and had sunk into a deep depression. It seemed he was not the only one who had received such missives and my heart bled for them. Not only had they endured the hell of war and sustained horrific injuries both to mind and body now they were being rejected by the ones they loved. I hoped poor Charlie and others like him would be able to put this nightmare behind them and ultimately meet someone who would love them for who they were and not what they now looked like. However, my hope had been dashed as a few weeks later en route to a clinic specializing in facial prosthetics Charlie had escaped from his carer and thrown himself down an embankment into the path of the London express putting himself out of his pain and misery.

Charles and I decided it was in the soldiers' best interests that they remain unaware of the tragic circumstances of their friend's demise. The rest of the staff agreed with our subterfuge.

We kept the newspapers out of sight and turned the wireless to a station that only played music. The explanation for his absence was that he had been sent to another facility, one which would cater much better to his needs.

The nights were the worst as the house resounded to the screams of the shell-shocked drawing me Bill or Charles to their sides in our efforts to calm and comfort them. On occasion, I would administer an injection which I had been instructed to do by the doctor who visited through the day this being the only way to relieve them of their horrors.

After one of those nights when I had sat bleary-eyed at breakfast leaving Charles in bed as he had a severe dose of bronchitis Hudson announced he had taken a telephone call from a military hospital in Balham. "It seems your ladyship," he had said, "that Lieutenant Williams is in a very bad way and is not expected to live. He is requesting the presence of his lordship."

I had been taken aback by this after wondering how Bunny had been faring but there was no chance of Charles visiting him. He could barely get out of bed and he also had a fever. I would have to go in his stead. Charles was appreciative of my offer to see his friend still unaware of the behavior he had exhibited towards me.

I had determined there would be nothing to gain by telling him. It was better to let sleeping dogs lie. With Charles' advice to stay safe and armed with directions from Hudson regarding the location of the hospital, I instructed Mrs. Keen regarding James and Charles' care. Then I was driven to the station by Bill, who had just enough petrol, for the next train leaving for London.

The journey was worse than the one I had taken with Mervyn. Squashed into a darkened compartment of kit bags and smelly weary soldiers the train stopped and started finally limping into Paddington after many hours. I was greeted by a scene of unimaginable devastation when I walked out of the station. There were hardly any buildings standing and those that were leaned at drunken angles ready to fall down at any minute. I found it hard to believe that London which had been a bustling city had been reduced to this. Picking my way through broken masonry and bricks I looked around for a cab and eventually one arrived.

"Where to lady?" the driver asked as I slid into the back seat which had a coating of fine dust.

"Balham, St James Military Hospital, thank you."

"Right you are. Visiting someone are you?"

"Yes, I am."

"Goodoh," he replied thankfully not requesting any more information. He seemed to be taking it all in his stride, even whistling a tune, he was probably by now desensitized to all the destruction and mayhem around him.

He drove off slowly threading his way around the bombed-out streets along which dazed pedestrians were walking and I wondered where they were going and if they had homes to return to.

"Here we are then, luv."

The driver pulled up outside a somber gray building in front of which a bored guard stood.

I thanked the driver and handed over the fare then approached the guard who directed me to the entrance and the location of the wards. I walked on and along corridors, redolent of antiseptic, gangrene and death.

I found him in ward three. There amidst the broken and dying he lay swathed in bandages with a drip in his arm, his pallor indicating the critical state he was in. This was confirmed by the sister who informed me he had suffered serious abdominal injuries and had lost a lot of blood. I was told that as I was not a relative I could stay only a few minutes. She reminded me then of a matron and I wondered what her fate was if she was still at the hospital and even if the hospital was standing, and what of my friends? It had been a while since we had contacted each other, as the lines of communication were not very reliable. Rachel still had not bothered to get in touch since that time when she had prevailed upon the goodness of Charles to rescue her from Berlin however that was my sister and I was used to her conduct.

I went over to a chair beside the bed and sat down. He sensed my presence and stirred. I looked at him. His face did not resemble in any way that nefarious character who had graced the rooms of Hagley Hall. This now was a man who had fought for his country and suffered just like all the other soldiers who were now at the final stages of their lives.

I leaned close to him and whispered.

"Bunny, can you hear me? It's Peggy, Charles' wife."

He opened his glazed eyes and tried to speak but I heard nothing.

I repeated what I had said now a little louder.

"I think it best that you leave Lieutenant to rest," announced the sister who was hovering around listening and watching.

I stood up to go but noticed that Bunny's finger was pointing to his jacket which was hanging on the knob of the cupboard.

"Your jacket, Bunny do you want it?"

He nodded.

I took it off the knob and placed it on the bed.

"Pocket," he gasped.

There was something he wanted me to find in the pocket.

Sister's anxiety was palpable and I knew she would soon have the security throw me out of the ward. I rummaged in the pockets and my fingers came upon what felt like an envelope which I pulled out.

"Is this it?" I asked him, "Is this what you want?"

"Charlie," he rasped. "Give to him."

"I insist you really must go now otherwise I shall have to call security," said sister the second time.

I pushed the envelope into my bag and left him there knowing it would be the final time I would see him alive.

I hurried from the hospital mystified about this tattered envelope and what it contained. Why was it so important that Bunny insisted I take it and give it to Charles? I located a tiny cafe a few streets away from the hospital. At a greasy table over a pot of stewed tea and a stale sandwich my curiosity became insurmountable. I had to know what was contained in the envelope Bunny had insisted on giving me. I took a good swig of tea and withdrew what was secreted inside. My eyes alighted on a legal document also tattered and mud-splattered having been dragged through the grime of the war. I was about to learn the shocking truth about Bunny, Lieutenant Williams. I read:

Let it be known that Henry Arthur Williams is the son of Lord Davenport the 4th of Hagley Hall, Bedfordshire, and one Grace Ivy Williams of Manchester. The sum of 50,000 pounds is held in trust by solicitors, Hemsley & Longbottom of 23 Bond Street, London until the said Henry Williams attains the age of 30 until and before which time he is never to divulge his parentage or to claim any rights to title and to do otherwise negates all claims to the said monies.

It was signed by Lord Davenport in the presence of a Justice of the Peace with a stamp affixed.

It was astounding! I could scarcely believe what I had just read, Bunny Williams was Charles' brother! Maybe that was why he had felt such an affinity with him. I wished I had something stronger than the stewed tea I was drinking. Bunny's past behaviour came to mind and I found myself excusing him. Obviously, he must have had psychological problems. It must have been such a burdensome secret to have kept all these years. I sat there in shock. I was uncertain about telling Charles what I had discovered. Would he want to know that he had a brother albeit a bastard? I would consider what to do on the train. I looked at my watch. I would have to hurry if I was to catch the 3.05. I knew it would be a slow journey and darkness would be falling when I arrived home. After all I had witnessed and discovered today it would be so wonderful to be back in the peace of the countryside in the arms of my beloved and to hold my darling baby once again.

I paid the bill and stepped out into the street. I did not hear or see it coming, this blast so fierce shaking the ground on which I stood and I was plunged into an abyss of darkness out of which there was no escape.

Chapter Twenty-Four

Many years have passed since that fateful day when a V1 rocket turned my world on its axis and left me seriously injured.

A wide area of Balham was destroyed including most of the military hospital where I had visited Bunny. My sight was lost due to the trauma of the blast and I spent many months at Luzerner Kantosspital a medical facility in Switzerland. My spine had been damaged and I was confined to a wheelchair. My memory of that day had been erased and it was not until a long time later when the miasma in my mind cleared and everything came back to me.

I had visited Bunny in the hospital. He had given me the document containing the momentous news that he was Charles' half-brother. However, Charles would never know this as a fatal strain of influenza had taken him before my memory was regained.

I decided never to divulge the secret to anyone and it is forever locked in my heart.

Charles had Bunny's body interred in the graveyard of the estate and on what would have been Bunny's 30th birthday when he received a posthumous award for bravery in battle. Now he and Charles are at rest side by side, brothers in death.

Charles would bring the boys to visit me in the hospital and how I looked forward to that. They would tell me how pretty the alps looked iced with snow while I hoped and prayed my vision would be restored and I could once again look upon the beauty of God's creation and on the faces of my children and Charles. My prayers were answered after my return to Hagley Hall when one morning I awoke and could see again. This was the cause of much celebration as Hudson sourced from the cellar a bottle of vintage champagne which had lain dormant throughout the war. It would the final time dear old Hudson discharged his duty as a few weeks later he passed away from a coronary occlusion.

The baton was passed to Henry who assumed the role of butler and he proved to be nearly as good as his predecessor. Mrs Keen stepped into the breach and together with Betty, a niece of matron's, I was well cared for.

I live on the estate albeit in the Dower House which befits a widow such as I. James, now the rightful heir is married to Ginny, a capable girl with a penchant for twin-sets and pearls. She and James have done a great job maintaining the estate and economising where they can. They have recently opened part of the House to the public every second Tuesday of the month and have turned the gardener's cottage into a gift shop and tea room. I think old Mullins would have approved although he would have swapped the tea for something stronger such as his favourite tipple.

Mervyn elected to study animal husbandry. He is married to Maryanne and they manage a piggery in Yorkshire. They have three little girls who delight in visiting their Granny in her big house. Mervyn seemed to possess an affinity with porkers. I remember not long after he came to us as a little child jumping in with our pigs after which nanny had to scrub the mud off him. He had certainly lived up to the adage, "happy as a pig in mud". Charles and I formally adopted him after his parents and siblings were killed by a bomb. He had a lucky escape as he was at the shop purchasing cigarettes for his mother when their house was obliterated. It had broken my heart that day when I delivered him to his mother amidst the war time moil and clamouring masses of the railway station.

Another dagger to pierce my heart was the loss of my friends Jean and her fiancé, Tims. They were en route to buy an engagement ring and were killed instantly when their bus took a direct hit by another of Hitler's bombs. The only saving grace was that they both were together and would not have known what was to befall them. I do not think that one could have survived without the other as I knew their love had been deep and abiding.

My other friends, Audrey and Edward survived the maelstrom continuing to drive ambulances during the Blitz and delivering babies in the most parlous conditions.

Auntie Eileen maintained a wonderful friendship with Cecily. Their relationship was forged in the Anderson shelter in which they hid from the bombs raining down on London. Thereafter they enjoyed attending exhibitions and art galleries and watching the latest films. However, their main interest and achievement had been locating foster parents for the Jewish children immigrating to Britain after the war. Charles had been one of a group who convinced the Home Secretary to amend a law in the House of Commons to issue visas enabling more children to escape from Germany. I often wonder if Cecily had ever been aware that her daughter's marriage to Charles had been nothing but a sham. If she had known that Diana had been enjoying a lesbian relationship and planned to take her new-born baby to live with her lover in that cottage in Kent.

My suspicions of Rachel and her lover being Nazi sympathisers had proved correct. Upon Rachel's return to Britain she was arrested and put on trial for passing information to the enemy. Lucinda was missing and presumed dead in the bombing of Berlin. Rachel received a period of six months incarceration in Holloway prison. I visited her once thinking she would appreciate seeing me, her only sister but I was mistaken as her contemptuous attitude had not been diluted by her imprisonment.

"Oh, has lady bountiful come to do her social duty?" She spat at me. Even the sight of my wheelchair did not elicit any sort of caring comment. There were no questions about my welfare or what had happened to me only vituperative outbursts from which I fled relieved to be with Charles driving away from her and that prison. She now lives in a secure facility on the outskirts of Oxford as she suffers from dementia and is unaware of who I am. I thought we might have become closer as siblings often do, the years mellowing any past grievances or rancour but, in our case, it was not to be.

I tire easily now and spend more time confined to my bed. My medications have been increased, Betty doling them out to me at regular intervals. I know my time on this earth is fast becoming limited and I will soon be with all the other souls who have gone before me. However, I have survived the vicissitudes of life. I have brought babies into the world, have had the love of a wonderful man and have seen my boys grow into fine men. I have travelled to places I never imagined I would visit and have had the privilege of living in beautiful Hagley Hall. I have survived the dark of the war and witnessed the dawn of a new era, a time of optimism and peace and for all that I am eternally grateful.

THE END

About the Author

From an early age, Annette was encouraged to write and was awarded several prizes for English.

A native of Sydney, Australia, she published a short story at the age of twelve.

She remained passionate to her writing, but the demands of raising a family left no time for writing.

Now retired, Annette has reignited her passion and has written six books with the seventh nearing completion.

Her interest lies in novels set around the periods of the first and second world wars.

Annette lives with her partner, Stephen, at Neutral Bay, a suburb on Sydney harbor in Australia. She has two sons, Mark and Brett, two grandsons, Jaime and Flynn and a sister, Maree.

The Dark Before the Dawn is her second published novel.